THE BLOWTOP

THE BLOWTOP

Alvin Schwartz

Copyright © 1948, 2001 by Alvin Schwartz

ALL RIGHTS RESERVED. Except for the quotation of short passages for the purposes of criticism and review, no part of this publication may be reproduced in whole or in part in any form.

Published in 2001 by Olmstead Press: Chicago, Illinois

Originally published in 1948 by The Dial Press: New York
Published in 1950 by Les Editions de L'Elan as *Le Cinglé*: Paris

Cover designed by Hope Forstenzer
Cover drawing by Jonas M. Land

Text designed and typeset by
Syllables, Hartwick, New York, USA

Printed and bound in the USA by
Rose Printing, Tallahassee, Florida

ISBN: 1-58754-007-X

Library of Congress Card Number: 2001089650

Editorial Sales Rights and Permission Inquiries should be addressed to:
Olmstead Press, 22 Broad Street, Suite 34, Milford, CT 06460
Email: Editor@lpcgroup.com

Manufactured in the United States of America
1 3 5 7 9 10 8 6 4 2

Substantial discounts on bulk quantities of Olmstead Press books are available to corporations, professional associations and other organizations. If you are in the USA or Canada, contact LPC Group, Attn: Special Sales Department, 1-800-626-4330, fax 1-800-334-3892, or email: sales@lpcgroup.com.

*I'm working on this canvas—The Woman, I call it.
And I get a little help from this bottle. Next thing happens,
I'm waking up in Washington Square Park. That's bad, no?*
—Willem deKooning

Introduction to the Second Edition

A depression-generated youthful anarchism coupled with equally youthful creative despairs had drawn me just three years before Pearl Harbor to Greenwich Village. Eight years later, my wife was celebrating her first one-man show at Peggy Guggenheim's ART OF THIS CENTURY, our first son was being born, and this book, *The Blowtop*, my first novel, appeared in print. It was January of 1948.

Of those artists I had come to know well, Jackson Pollock was convinced he was the painter protagonist in this novel. He recognized, I think, the general outlines of the personality, although my real model, a less well-known painter, similarly demonstrated that fierce self immolating drive to absorb into his work the continuing agony of a world still recovering from war. Both Jackson and Attilio Salemme, the other painter, had become part of that drive to eliminate representationalism, and somehow take up into their canvasses and transfigure the detritus of World War II. They were among some two hundred very different painters whose work came to be known collectively as Abstract Expressionism. In time, they formed an annex to Greenwich Village in the little Long Island village of Springs, the poor man's side of the upscale township of East Hampton.

For many of these artists the conjoined agonies of fame and death by suicide have been well documented and includes names like Pollock, Gorky and Rothko— a conjunction that I came to recognize largely because I found myself, in my own struggles, living in such revealing personal and artistic propinquity to those caught in these extremes. *The Blowtop* was a recognition and a celebration of their struggles, especially as they meshed with my own. I confronted in this early work a state that was essentially despair. Simultaneously, Jean-Paul Sartre and the French Existentialists were doing the same thing in France, and indeed were taking on despair as the true human condition as expounded by Sartre's publication of what I chose to call his bible of depression—*La Nausée*. On this point, during an interview with Harvey Breit of the *NY Times* Book Section, I suggested an existentialism rather different from Sartre's essentially Marxist oriented movement. I spoke of transcendence. But this was not so much an idea to me. It was *The Blowtop*'s own distinct fictional vision and emerged strongly in the following scene:

> Giordano shook his head. He appeared struggling to lift himself above some level of obsession. "What is it? What is painting?" he demanded. "I'll tell you. It's my direct struggle with reality—with things, with space." He paused and seemed to make an effort to continue. "Without it, I wouldn't be able to purify, to know closely the things that are left over." He stalked toward Archie, his face taut. "Don't you see it?"
>
> Archie regarded him in numbed silence. Giordano turned again to the painting, his voice rising. "Look at it! Slime and sediment!" He brought his hands together in a gesture of squeezing something. "Wrung out of life to make living clean enough to endure. What a monstrosity!

Look hard at it! Isn't it horrible? There's all the filth of existence right before your eyes! God!"

Now, fifty-two years later, the novel seems even more compelling than when I wrote it. Because now I know very well the value of what Giordano called "the things that are left over." In rereading it recently, I found myself less surprised than I was when *The Blowtop,* under the title *Le Cinglé,* published in Paris by Les Editions de l'Elan in 1950, became a best seller.

Earlier, in New York's quirky world of book publishing, well before *The Blowtop* appeared in print, the owner of Dial Press returned from the war, a victim of what in those days was called "shell-shock." For reasons known only to himself, he deliberately killed all the books his Executive Vice President, George Joel had been handling. He spitefully put a mystery jacket on *The Blowtop* and thus made sure that the real sense of that work would be difficult indeed for reviewers to discover. And then he killed himself. Fortunately, that interview in the *NY Times* caught the attention of the French publisher.

In addition, the *Saturday Review of Literature* seemed to recognize beneath the false covers that there was something different about *The Blowtop*. Since it was presented as a mystery, the *Saturday Review* did run it in their mystery column at the top of the page. Under their regular heading: "Time, Place & Sleuth," they wrote most dispassionately: "Sudden death of reefer seller in Greenwich Village Saloon mildly interests police and dislocates lives of pedlar's acquaintances." But then, under the heading "Summing Up," they stated: "'Routine' crime is basis of penetrating and well-written analysis of several depressing but amply realized characters, 'artistic' and otherwise." And in their summary column, Verdict, where each reviewed mystery was usually characterized in very brief epithets such as Good; Time-passer; Plenty-tough; For the shudder-shelf; Diverting; amd the like, they offered a rather unusual one word summary for *The Blowtop*. "Impressive."

Well, it was something, but not enough for the book to go anywhere. And it didn't. There was only the most meager of consolations from George Joel, offered at the time he returned "all right, title and interest" in the book to me. "I thought you'd like to know," he said somewhat sheepishly, "that *The Blowtop* has become a kind of cult book at Columbia University." That was early in 1948.

This bit of information was meaningless to me at the time. It was to take several years before I learned that sometime in the mid-fifties the initiating personalities of the "Beat" movement. Jack Kerouac and Allen Ginsberg had begun their long discussions while students at Columbia on a revived kind of Bohemia precisely in 1948, and that those discussions involved a special focus on both abstract expressionism and French existentialism. Given these parallels, certain friends of mine found it easy to insist that Kerouac and Ginsberg had not only been influenced by *The Blowtop*, they had made it their bible.

Of course, the parallels, while interesting, didn't prove very much. I had never regarded the Beat movement as truly Bohemian, but rather, taking the original sense of "beat," it struck me that Ginsberg and Kerouac at Columbia appeared to have affected a kind of weariness, rather than having tried to instigate a new Bohemianism. That assumed "weariness" seemed little more than literary nostalgia for the old Greenwich Village and its now dissipating Bohemia. It's even possible that *The Blowtop*—which they very likely had read just because they were around during its cult status at Columbia —played some role in nurturing that nostalgia. It seems to me too that even the work of the poet William Carlos Williams, a clear influence on Ginsberg himself, only began to show itself after the Williams legend had become text-book material by the mid-fifties. In other words. during the growth process Ginsberg's poetry went through, emerging from a sentimental and derivative 18th century diction in 1949:—

> Take my love, it is not true,
> So let it tempt no body new;
> Take my lady, she will sigh
> For my bed where'er I lie...

to a more modern idiom as much as six years later, Williams may simply have been recalled as part of Allen's schooling in newer styles of poetry.

By 1955, Ginsberg. in some ways a slow starter, was long gone from Columbia. And only then did he finally produce his great epic poem, *Howl,* with its rich echoes of Williams. Also by then Greenwich Village itself was well into a post-war real-estate boom that had dispersed most of its artistic inhabitants into places like Soho and the East Village.

The new American prosperity, sparked by long pent-up demand, the GI bill, the ubiquity of the automobile, the efflorescence of the new Levittowns had transmuted into full-blown suburbia. Bohemian types were completely displaced by the daily commuter, the new middle-class family, the organization man and, as lamented toward the end of the fifties by David Reisman in *The Lonely Crowd,* and the authors of books like *The Organization Man* and *The Man in the Gray Flannel Suit,* a dull, somewhat supine and conformist society. For Ginsberg, it was time to trot out the old Bohemian and revolutionary spirit as he had learned it from Williams.

By this time too the idea of "beat" had changed from its original sense of weariness to what the *Encyclopedia Brittanica* calls "beatitude." It had to be something like that. How express a poetic sense of value or, for Kerouac, the significance of sheer wanderlust without some reference point of value. In Ginsberg's case, certainly, as his poetic skills developed with such striking energy, the only direction that led from weariness was for the word "beat" to become a standin for beatitude. I would even suggest that in the transit from weariness to beatitude, it was a little like going from bad lassitude to good lassitude.

Personally, I came to admire a lot of Ginsberg's work after *Howl*. I never saw in Kerouac much more than a troubled and somewhat mediocre talent. But apart from the movement itself which took on new dimensions as it gathered up a variety of talented writers such as Ferlinghetti and Burroughs and numerous others, my interest here is to make clear the position of *The Blowtop* and in what way it may have influenced the "beat" movement.

First, I needed to establish that *The Blowtop* came out of the personal experience that encountered very directly the kind of Bohemia that flourished in the forties, and most powerfully immediately after the war. As a novel, it plunges head-on into the drives that led so many abstract expressionists to use their work as a way of absorbing the personal detritus the war had left with them. In the self-destruction of my artist protagonist, Giordano, a reader might well come to understand how that same burdened vision destroyed some of the best of the abstract expressionists. They were an influential group, but largely a transitional one. In their passing, many small and inarticulated movements have been taking shape with, as yet, no clear direction.

In expressing the despair that marked many aspects of abstract expressionism, *The Blowtop* with its own existential visions of that despair may not be quite the "beat" novel some have called it, including, oddly enough, the Canadian used book dealer who charged me an absurdly high price for a copy in good condition because he had it classified as "an early beat novel." Certainly, such a classification can't be made on the basis of despair alone, as Sartre's existentialism treats despair. But in the notion of transcendence which I can now see so firmly woven into the story, it may indeed be not just the earliest "beat" novel, but the first of the beats to move toward that notion of inner beatitude that ultimately was to define the "beats" raison d'etre.

In reviewing this early novel of mine after not having seen it for decades, I find it rather marvelous in the way the story reveals the possibility of transcendence. I had somehow attained in that youthful work a vision that only today is becoming an active element in my awareness and the reality in which it subsists. Or what I then called "the things that are left over."

Alvin Schwartz
Aug 2, 2000
Chesterville, Ontario

Chapter 1

In the early evening of one of those spring days whose charms more purposive souls could scarcely resist, Archie Grau, a waifish-looking individual of thirty, standing indecisively on the corner of Seventh Avenue and Sheridan Square, made up his mind not to return home to work on the book he was helping to write for a certain Brankowski, a pedagogue whose literary ambitions exceeded his talent for expressing them. Having made this decision, Archie was suddenly faced with such limitless freedom that the problem of enjoying it became as burdensome as the duty he had postponed.

Consequently, he began to walk, not in order to arrive at any particular place, but as though the mere act of setting himself in motion could enlarge the area of possible events which might invite his participation. He went slowly south along Seventh Avenue, his head held slackly forward to compensate for the shuffling gait that threw his weight well back on his heels and made his shoes scuff unevenly on the pavement. The tweed suit that hung stiffly over his thin frame seemed independent of the body it covered, as though it were a container rather than an article of clothing.

Occasionally, as he walked, he turned his head in a desultory near-sighted quest for a familiar face. Finally, he found himself standing before the open doorway of the 16 Bar, smallest of the motley row of night spots wedged within the one-block area between Sheridan Square and Barrow Street.

Withdrawing the cigarette from his mouth, he dropped it, trod it out, and turned in toward the soft exposure of the amber bulbs. The bar was crowded. Two rotary fans slung from the low ceiling churned through the fetid smoke-filled air.

Archie pushed through the crowd. An archway separated the bar from the table section at the rear. He reached a relatively uncongested spot under the archway without discovering a single familiar face. But he tentatively picked out a red-haired girl for a second glance. Two others, nearby and looking like sisters drew his attention for a moment. However, his hunger was not equal to the effort required to satisfy it.

The table section was nearly empty. The bandstand in the corner was unoccupied but the musicians had left their instruments. They would probably return shortly. He pushed his way back toward the entrance. Someone coming through the door in the opposite direction thrust him against a fat girl perched on a stool at the bar. Two lean sailors, one on either side, arched over her in conversation like twin ears on a shaving mug. Next to one of the sailors, a man turned from the bar and, in trying to squeeze out toward the door, forced Archie into the empty space he had left.

Archie remained in this unsought anchorage, staring at an empty beer glass that stood before him on the stained walnut counter. The crowd milled behind him. The sailor on his left placed an arm across the fat girl's shoulder. She giggled as the sailor overturned her drink. The bartender slopped his rag over the wet spot. The sailor apologized. The bartender dropped the rag under the counter. His large puppy-brown eyes, which seemed on the point of liquefy-

Chapter 1

ing rotated toward the sailor from some firmly fixed point on his square, rock-like face.

"You guys should learn to keep your balance on dry land."

Archie suddenly regretted coming. He thought of leaving. But he finally responded to an impulse that required less effort than thrusting his way through the crowd to reach the door. He dropped a dime on the counter and slapped his palm over it.

"Give me a beer, Carlo."

The bartender's eyes expanded. "When did you come in? I never even noticed you."

"Just got here," Archie said. "Maybe you work too hard."

Carlo swept his forehead with the back of his hand. "You're telling me. Beer?"

"Beer," Archie said. He watched Carlo stoop beneath the bar for a glass.

"How's Fred?" Carlo asked.

"You know Fred," Archie said. "He leads a complicated life." He tasted the beer.

"What's complicated about chasing broads?" Carlo said. "He should have this job. One week, I give him—that's all." He thrust out a finger.

"Always complaining," Archie said. "You've got enough dough for your old age. Why don't you quit? You can chase broads too. It's a free country."

"Yeah," Carlo said. "You should know."

"Hey!" The sailor next to Archie rapped on the bar. "How about a fresh drink for the lady?"

"You see," said Carlo. "Not even time to breathe."

The sailor grunted and clutched at Archie's shoulder. "Ask him if he'd like to trade jobs."

Carlo poured a drink from a bottle of rye. "You got a deal, bud. At least you got a healthy life. Trouble is, you don't know when you're well off."

"Healthy!" the sailor exclaimed. "Yeah, but it ain't living."

Carlo put the drink in front of the fat girl. "Here," he said. "You look healthy."

The fat girl giggled. Archie took another sip of beer. There wasn't much doing, he thought. He ought to be leaving. He could still manage to get that section written by morning. He'd had plenty of sleep. He could probably work through the night. He would give himself five more minutes, he decided. Then he'd head straight for home. He tilted the glass up to finish his beer. Someone put a hand on his shoulder.

Archie put the glass down and turned around. It was Phil White, a local hanger-on and occasional peddler of marijuana, from whom Archie had sometimes purchased reefers. As it happened, Archie had been discussing Phil earlier that evening and his appearance now brought to Archie's mind certain facts the other could confirm. He started to say hello. But he still hadn't made a sound when his first recognition was superseded by a disturbing discovery. The face at which he stared had abruptly gone out of focus with his own familiar mental image of Phil White. He was looking at Phil White, but there was something in Phil's face that he had never seen and never conceivably could have seen before. The mouth was open and was trying to articulate something and a hand was pointing to that idiotically gaping mouth as if in tortured explanation of the astonishing wordlessness.

Archie instinctively drew back. His spine struck the ridge of the bar. Phil's convulsively working features were losing identity like wax over a flame. Simultaneously they were thrusting so close that the head no longer balanced on the rest of the body.

"Hey—" Archie exclaimed, "what's the matter with—"

But before he could finish the sentence, Archie shriveled under Phil's clawing fingers which groped frenziedly

Chapter 1

down his chest in a blind, futile attempt to support that suddenly fluid, crumpling form. Then Phil struck the floor, not with a single, direct impact but as though he were being absorbed into it like a glob of jelly on a piece of bread. Archie gaped. Phil lay shapelessly at his feet.

He tried to tell himself that Phil was drunk. He tried to ignore the spasm in his throat. He made a terrible effort to control himself so that he could lift Phil to his feet again. But he couldn't bring himself to stoop over and touch that form in its twisted aspect of decay, suddenly more vegetable than human—fungus and not flesh. He was still fighting his revulsion when the sailor next to him slipped his arm from the fat girl's shoulder and caught Phil below the armpits, hauling him roughly erect.

"All right, mate. Snap out of it."

The sailor shook his limp burden. There was no response other than the further dropping of that sagging mouth in a face that had already lost all of its individual character.

"Come on." The sailor was losing patience. "You use your feet for standing, not your face."

Carlo's granite jaw thrust truculently across the bar. The spongy brown eyes sopped up the scene which had produced on the rest of his face an expression of bewildered innocence.

"What's the matter?" he shouted. "What've you got there?"

The sailor was too busy grappling with his burden. It was Archie who answered. He pointed to Phil's dangling figure which the sailor was shaking to elicit some response.

"It's Phil."

"Wake up, you rum-head," the sailor said. "I ain't no nurse." He released one arm from its clumsy hold so that the inert form depended entirely from the hand grasping the collar at the back of the neck. He was about to slap at the blanched, gaping face when his eyes lifted in panic.

The sailor was staring at his own fingers. "Christ!" he exclaimed. "This guy ain't drunk." He held out his hand. "Look! Blood!"

The fat girl, through a dexterous shift of her center of gravity, managed to slip sideways off her stool. The bovine face veered for an instant from its fixed expression of placidity toward some indefinable and never quite attained sign of emotion. The amorphous features stirred weakly with all the response that stupidity could contrive. She gazed with absurd and uncomprehending serenity at the sailor and his flaccid burden.

"What happened to him?"

The second sailor thrust her aside. "How does he know, you dope? Let me have a look, Eddie."

"I think he's dead," the sailor named Eddie said.

Archie's nostrils flattened with an involuntary inhalation. His heart went faster. Something hard formed in his throat.

The crowd began to reshift and reassemble around the center of excitement. Archie braced his heel against the rail and surged forward against the pressure that would have pinned him back against the ridge of the bar. He saw Carlo charging around the end of the bar and plunging through the milling spectators. his big body like a stone dropping irresistibly through water.

The bartender's plunge caused a displacement, forcing someone in front of Archie and cutting off his view. His sense of suffocation increased. Flattening himself against the bar, he inched along toward the outside of the mob in the direction of the door. He didn't quite understand why, but he wished to be nearer the door.

Now, standing on the edge of the crowd, he was better able to take account of things. His view was impeded but he had a desperate need to know and to know immediately whether Phil was really dead.

Probably, he thought, someone had slugged Phil. Or maybe Phil had fallen and cracked his skull. It was possible

Chapter 1

to walk around for quite some time after sustaining a head injury before anything happened.

Above the others, a new voice now rose in distinct authority like a dancer bolting unexpectedly from the chorus. "Let me through. I'm a doctor."

A hush descended on the onlookers. There was a shifting of position that began somewhere at the core of the ragged circle and spread slowly outward, allowing Archie a momentary glimpse of the second sailor, forcing an opening into the compressed area of action.

"Let this guy through. He's a doctor."

Carlo's voice poured more efficiently into the pronounced lull. "Come on. Clear out."

Archie, again, without realizing what he was doing, started to move automatically toward the door. Almost at the threshold, he noticed with embarrassment that no one else was obeying Carlo's injunction. His isolate act compelled him to take stock of his own relation to the event, beginning with that sailor who might even at this moment see him poised for leave-taking and who unquestionably had observed that he knew Phil to the extent of being able to point him out and repeat his name to the bartender. This recalled something even more disturbing. Archie remembered that Phil had been trying to tell him something just before he collapsed. Anyway, why was he trying to leave? What had gotten into him? He started to push his way back through the crowd again.

Then he heard the doctor's voice for the second time. He listened and found himself trying to feel whatever it was that such words were always meant to evoke and never quite succeeded in doing.

"He's dead," the doctor said. After a pause, he added in shocked tones. "He's been shot. There's a bullet wound in his head."

Archie's eyes began to water. His head dropped furtively below the general line of vision. The announcement had been transmuted into a kind of accusation, a sourceless and overwhelming sensation that his reason was unable to resist. He blinked rapidly and shook his head in an effort to escape the ridiculous feeling of culpability. In aimless anxiety, he wiped his hands on the sides of his jacket, shifting his weight from one foot to the other until the silence nurturing his discomfort was shattered by Carlo's voice:

"Who shot him?"

It was not a question addressed to the doctor or even to anyone present who might have been a witness as much as it was a direct outburst of injured feelings, a demand that the wielder of the gun, now that the practical joke had served its purpose, step forward and reveal himself. The absurdity of the demand mitigated the shock of the announcement preceding it. The tension in the crowd was broken. The silence was expunged by the excited voices that were all at once released like greyhounds after the starting signal.

"I didn't hear no shot," said a man standing at Archie's left.

"Maybe it was done with a silencer."

A woman shouted hysterically. "Somebody send for the police. Why doesn't somebody send for the police?"

"Does anybody here know who the guy is?"

It was this last question which stimulated Archie into a swift, uncontemplated thrust toward the center of the scene, lifting himself bodily out of his fantasy of guilt, dispelling it in the very act of tugging at Carlo's arm, like a child seeking the attention of an absent-minded parent.

"He tried to tell me something before he fell," Archie said, as though this fact contained an inner significance which Carlo could somehow reveal. "Only he didn't say a word," Archie added. "I guess I ought to stick around."

Carlo's face was lifted to the ceiling in martyr-like resignation and his eyes appeared to be seeking some invisible being dwelling in the smoke-laden area between those two rotary fans which turned uninterruptedly overhead.

Chapter 1

"It was a first-class night," he said. "Why does this have to happen to me?"

"Shouldn't I stick around?" Archie inquired.

Carlo, in response to that insistent tugging, turned reluctantly from his invisible communicant to glower at Archie.

"What do you want to get mixed up in this for? Are you crazy? Go on—beat it while you have a chance."

Archie's mouth snapped shut. His eyes seemed to diminish in size. "Well, you know how it is—"

But Carlo had turned away to speak to the sailor named Eddie who had just phoned the police.

"They're on the way over now. Christ. I seen guys killed. Why is this so different?"

Several people took this as a signal to exit and the crowd rapidly began to lose its organic identity. Small groups evolved from the process of fragmentation, some drifting toward the door, others lingering in morbid attendance on whatever further turns the lethal drama had yet to take.

Archie, severed from the event by Carlo's splenetic dismissal, became the last of a group that straggled out. He presented a contemplative frown to those who stood watching outside. It was an effort to mask the increasing panic which he feared had become quite noticeable in him. Placing his hands in his pockets with calculated nonchalance, he stepped off the curb and crossed to the other side of the street, walking with an odd inelegant shuffle, an effort at relaxed informality, past the old buildings whose darkened windows faced each other across the cobblestones.

Soon, he was thinking, the police would be arriving on the murder scene. He conjured up out of cinematic tag ends the manner in which they would take over, visualizing the medical examiner bent over the body, the official photographer making his flashbulb shots, the plainclothesman with the notebook, constantly scribbling whatever data happened to belong to violent death from the specialized point of view of the law.

Out of this imagined scene rose a new fear, a threat so startling as to thrust from his mind any concern he still nurtured for the other more nameless menaces of the evening. The police, he suddenly realized, would investigate the marijuana angle. Phil's patrons might all be contacted for questioning. And in the dresser drawer at home were still several "sticks of tea," several unenjoyed proffers of mild illegality which would have to be gotten rid of at once.

It was not the "tea" that disturbed him, however, since its disposal presented no real problem. That same drawer contained an additional and far more serious item of dereliction. How could it possibly have slipped his mind up until this moment? Something would have to be done right away. There was no time to lose.

As he arrived at the next corner, he turned to look back at the 16 Bar now two blocks away. A quick glance reassured him. He crossed the street and continued on toward home, walking as rapidly as caution would permit, since at this point he dared not risk being seen leaving the 16 Bar too hurriedly. Above all, he must avoid provoking suspicion. From this moment on, every move would have to be made with circumspection.

Chapter 2

Archie's new fear had its origin in certain events that had occurred that same afternoon, just a few hours prior to the death of Phil White. Having risen late that day, Archie had had difficulty in bringing himself to work. After some tentative efforts at the typewriter, he had finally given up and abandoned himself to the armchair that stood near his work table in the dining room. For some time he had stared somberly across the room at the dust-stained window through which the fading light filtered. He had felt content to watch the gradual invasion of darkness, as though, with the increase of shadow, his palpable self could diminish, permitting him to become one with the room and the graying objects it contained. The window, being open near the top, admitted an intermittent breeze which infused the stillness with life. The dangling blind shuddered discreetly. A loose strand of hair oscillated above his forehead. The sheet of paper obtruding brightly from the black mass of the typewriter gave off an occasional rustle so that the lines of type visible above the roller danced, creating the illusion of moving independently and chaotically across the white surface.

Leaning forward in his chair, he could still distinguish some of the sentences he had been busily constructing until, beguiled by the afternoon's foretaste of spring, that redolence in the air of caprice and nostalgia, he had surrendered to the intimacy of his reveries.

But his mood was far from tranquil. He would have preferred to be roaming the streets, romantically available for whatever encounter might come his way. Still, his work could not be wholly disdained. By remaining at least within the proximity of the typewriter, neither actually at work nor actually taking his pleasure outside, he could keep his conscience at bay.

As he peered across at the table, laboring to decipher the scarcely visible words on the partially filled sheet jutting from the machine, the sentences ran together idiotically, clogging in his brain. The meaningless exercise exaggerated an expression that was characteristic. He had long ago acquired that look of a man who gazes directly and constantly into the sun in embattled denial of its overwhelming brightness. His face had the appearance of having been parched and dried, producing the shrewd lines that parenthetically enclosed his mouth. A fleshy knob at the tip of his nose extended toward his thin extruding lips so that the organs of smelling and kissing seemed intent on exercising their functions on each other, adding to his myopic intensity an air of profound preoccupation.

As he stared at the typewriter, wondering whether to resume his interrupted task, he experienced a growing resentment. His determination to complete another section of the Brankowski book by morning was scarcely nearer realization than it had been twelve hours before. Why was it he could never break through the problem of discipline? His memory, awakened by the insolent breeze that had now completely invaded the room, stirred up fragments of the past, the ache of abandoned dreams. From the grandiose aspirations he had enjoyed at school to this room and the drudgery of working anonymously on an elementary science text—how long had it been? So that Brankowski with his rimless glasses and his foul breath might satisfy his pedagogical ambitions with a minimum of intellectual effort, Archie Grau, at the age of thirty, continued to lay aside his own vast projects to labor grudgingly and obscurely on a work in which he could never possibly have been interested.

How quickly time ran out! If he were to accomplish anything at all in life, he could no longer afford postponements. He began to recall previous decisions to focus his energies on his own work by eschewing those distractions to which he was constantly drawn. He had made starts of one kind and another. He had prepared schedules for himself, announcing to his friends that he would no longer be available to them as before. He had on several occasions referred to plans that were in the making to withdraw for some indefinite period to write a book. Sometimes he had suggested that the book in prospect was a novel. Sometimes he had spoken vaguely of a volume of criticism. He had also hinted at some original political views on which he had already collected notes and which the approaching period of hibernation would enable him to put in order.

His thoughts produced an inaudible sigh. How could he work in such a state? What a detestable existence!

He allowed his head to sag against the cushioned back of the chair. The gloom continued to gather in the room. The shadows merged into uniform obscurity. From the kitchen came the abrupt hum of the refrigerator. Archie tried to wrench his thoughts to other things. Various images rose successively in his mind. The darkness swelled, engulfing the familiar forms. He sat immersed in his world of phantoms.

A series of sounds: the fall of footsteps, the creaking of a door, the echo of floorboards now reached him distantly, merging with his preoccupations. An electric switch clicked. The room burst from obscurity. His eyes recoiled from the sudden rushing brightness of the overhead light. He started from the chair in momentary panic, then arrested himself to turn and peer through the dancing incandescence, making out after a moment the familiar figure of Fred, his literary partner and roommate, with his back to the still open door, his hand moving in a descending curve from the wall switch.

Fred's heavy face took shape under the dispersing glare. His lips moved, forming an oval of astonishment as he recognized Archie.

"Oh! I didn't think anybody was home."

"I didn't hear you come in," Archie said. "You look tired. I was trying to work."

Fred settled heavily on the wooden chair next to the table and gazed at the sheet in the typewriter. "You didn't go very far, did you?"

"Spring sneaked up on me and slugged me. Christ, I can't do that crap anymore. I need a vacation." He eyed his collaborator apologetically. "Maybe you'd finish this section for me?"

"The hell I will. I did my stint." Fred glowered at the floor, then rolled his head back, covering his mouth in a yawn. "I'm shot," he articulated, forcing the words through the gulp of air. He dropped a hand to his knee. A faint smile lifted his sagging features. "I wore myself out exchanging gossip with Dave Weiss in Washington Square Park. He's full of angles, that guy. He's lined up a string of night spots on Twenty-third Street for a camera route. He's got three girls already. If we finish the Brankowski in time, maybe we can invest a couple of hundred. It looks like a good deal."

"Not me," Archie said. "I told you this is my last hack job for a while. I'm going to need that dough to live on while I do some of my own work for a change."

Fred shrugged. "I've heard that before."

"This time I mean it."

"Well, I'll try to reconcile myself to the end of our beautiful marriage. It's such a wrench, you know. If it didn't happen every two weeks, I'd be worried."

"You'll see," Archie said. "If I don't get started sometime, I never will. I'm thirty already. What have I got to show for it?"

Fred had risen and started toward the adjoining room. At the threshold, he turned. "So, I'm thirty-two. Do you see me tearing my hair out over it? What's ambition? There are more interesting experiences in life than a literary career. Like sleep. I feel like stretching out for a week. But try to get that part finished and wake me at midnight. I'll do the next section and deliver the whole batch to Brankowski in the morning, although it'll probably kill him, our being ahead of schedule for a change."

Archie gazed distastefully at the typewriter. "If I only had some benzedrine," he said. "I—"

The broken sound of the buzzer interrupted him. He exchanged a pained look with Fred.

"Who's that?"

"Company," Fred commented as he pressed the wall button that released the downstairs door. "If we weren't so popular, maybe we'd get somewhere. That's your trouble, believe me. You've got too much charm. Make yourself detestable and you'll be able to get work done."

They heard heavy footsteps ascending the stairs. "It doesn't sound like a woman," Archie said. "Work or no work, an evening like this was made for romance."

Fred opened the door and looked out. The pale sharp-featured face of a man rose above the stair-rail. Eyes pallid and bemused fixed on Fred. The indrawn mouth stretched in a meager smile.

"Hello," the visitor said. His voice had a peculiar lightness as though the breath that expelled it scarcely existed. Yet the sound was clear and grotesquely penetrating, like an echo. Reaching the landing, the visitor waved a gnarled hand that seemed to move mechanically owing to the constraining snugness of the black serge suit that pinched shoulders and sleeves as though the wearer had arrived at a peculiar rigidity out of an effort to achieve neatness.

"Well! Giordano!" Fred exclaimed. "Welcome to Grub Street. You're just in time to ruin my nap and wreck Archie's work. Come in."

"The stuff you do isn't work," Giordano said, stepping past Fred into the room. His words fell lightly, without intonation. Nodding to Archie, he continued: "What is work? You think any drudgery a man undertakes can be called work? You don't understand anything."

Archie pulled himself from the armchair and stretched his arms above his head. He groaned with the effort. Then, leaning back against the table, he pointed to the double bed placed against the far wall.

"Sit down before you start lecturing. Allow us to show a little hospitality. I haven't seen you in two weeks. Where've you been hiding?"

Giordano drew a pipe from his pocket and pressed the loose fragments of tobacco into the bowl. "Working," he said. He sat down on the edge of the bed.

Fred straddled the wooden chair and rested his forearms across the back. "So, tell us. If work's not drudgery, what is it? I'm looking for a new attitude to bolster the sagging morale of my partner here. He wants to quit again."

"I've been painting steadily for three weeks. That's work," Giordano said.

"Work to a painter," Fred remarked. "Making colored mud pies on a piece of canvas. So far, I'm not impressed."

Giordano held a match to his pipe. "That's because you don't know what work is." He forced quantities of smoke from the charred bowl. "I learned about work when I was in the nut-house. That was the first time I ever seriously thought about it. It was after the first horror of being there, the baths, the shocks, the whole works. I tried to understand how it had happened. There was a line I crossed somewhere. And if I could cross it, why wasn't it a line that anybody could cross? What was it? I thought about it for days, sitting there in a funk. Meanwhile, I was at the mercy of the whole sadistic institution. There was nothing I could do. I had to learn to take whatever came along or it would have been worse." Giordano's face grew painfully reminiscent. "It was that way as long as I was alone with myself. I was stuck with my own aches and pains, with my own misery. So it began to become clear to me. A man isn't made for leisure. He's a creative animal. He has to work. Only—" He pointed toward the typewriter. "That stuff—that's not what I mean by work. That's still being left alone with your own misery. You see what I mean?"

Archie, resting on the arm of the overstuffed chair, nodded. "You're really talking."

"Work," Giordano continued, "has to be something bigger than your own misery. Bigger than you." He made a sweeping gesture with the pipe.

Fred pulled himself from his chair and let his arms fall to his sides in irritated dismissal of the subject. "I've heard the theory before," he said. "From psychiatrists. If one of them can tell me how to make a living without drudgery, I'd listen to his nonsense."

"It's an interesting idea," Archie said. "Leaving out the question of work. The idea of keeping hold with something bigger than yourself—it's ancient, but still good."

"The two of you," Fred said. "I'll tell you what you're suffering from. It's spring fever. It's a sentimental time of the year."

"Sentimental?" Giordano queried. "Not me. I don't feel spring anymore." He stood up, his eyes moist, his thin face thrust forward like the blade of a hatchet. "Three weeks of solid painting," he said. "Just buried in it. I'm getting closer and closer." His voice sharpened, sounding as if a taut string had been plucked on a violin. "Do you know what it is that's bigger than life?"

Archie watched him apprehensively. "You're really worked up tonight." He turned to Fred. "Look at him. The calmest guy in the world usually. He acts as if he's about to take off."

Giordano relaxed, watching them with a sudden gay flirtatiousness. His eyes flickered back and forth. "No," he said. "I *am* upset. I'm furious. But it's something entirely different. A very tawdry business. I've been swindled out of nine bucks by Phil White, the bastard."

Fred smiled. "This sounds good. So that's what's behind all the nonsense about life and work. Learn a lesson," he remarked to Archie. "Always look beneath the surface of things and you'll find the vulgar truth. What happened?"

"I'll tell you what happened," Giordano said. "He comes over to the house yesterday. He's got a load of tea. 'Wonderful stuff,' he says. You know how he gives it a build-up. I tell him I don't use much. I've got to lay off the reefers. If I smoke too much, I get way out. I go off somewhere. I don't want to get that way again. So I offer to take an ounce. You know what he lets me have it for? A bargain! Nine bucks!"

"That's cheap," Archie said.

"For good tea, it's cheap," Giordano admitted. "All right. I took the stuff in good faith. Why shouldn't I? I've known Phil a long time. He's regular. He's supposed to be a buddy of mine. What happens? I'll tell you. As soon as Phil leaves, I light up. Nothing happens. I light another one. Still nothing. Well, why go into details? I thought at first it was me. Maybe I couldn't get high anymore. Anyway, I take a closer look at the stuff. Catnip! Pure catnip! It wasn't even adulterated. That I could understand. But one hundred percent catnip! It burns me up!"

"So you were stabbed in the back," Fred said, laughing.

"It's not funny. I'll kill the bastard if I get my hands on him. In the meantime, I've been dying for a stick. That's why I came over. You don't happen to have any around, do you?"

"So that's your real reason for coming over. And all along," Archie said, "I thought it was our charm." He looked at Fred. "How about it?"

Fred shrugged. "I guess we can spare one stick." He opened the top drawer of the dresser which stood at the head of the bed. Giordano stared curiously over his shoulder. With an exclamation, he suddenly reached in and pulled out a gleaming .22 pistol from the drawer.

"What's this?"

"Take it easy," Fred admonished. "It's loaded."

Giordano hefted it in his palm. "A handy little gadget. What's it for?"

"Oh, just one of those things." He watched Giordano restore the gun and then lean back against the drawer, closing it.

"How about lending it to me?" Giordano suggested. "I could scare the hell out of Phil White and get back my nine bucks."

"Forget Phil White." Fred pulled Giordano away from the dresser and handed him a stick of tea. "Here, this ought to keep you happy."

Archie would have found it difficult to explain exactly why he and Fred had purchased that gun. A friend had found it lying in the grass in Washington Square Park two years ago. Five dollars had given them possession of that polished, compact instrument of aggression. Thus they had cheaply equipped themselves for dangers too indefinite to be mentioned, real enough to require protection against and still too nebulous to demand anything more than the mere suggestion of violence that tiny, ineffectual weapon contained. Their purchase had been little more than an exaggerated exercise of prudence. The gun had never been intended for use. But they enjoyed possessing it almost as a lover may cherish a scented letter or a lock of hair.

Giordano drew out his breast pocket handkerchief, carefully folded the reefer in it, and stuffed it into the side pocket of his jacket.

"Thanks," he said. "This makes me feel better."

"Are you going?" Archie said, watching him move toward the door.

"I've got to get back," Giordano said. "If I stay away too long, if I let myself get tangled up with the outside world, in this crazy spring—" He paused and seemed to glare at them. "No, I can't afford to lose it. I'm standing right on the threshold now. I can't explain. It's bigger than being alive and letting yourself go nuts in this insidious weather. Oh, what the hell!" He suddenly pulled open the door, stepped outside and was gone.

"I'll see you," Archie called out belatedly.

Fred slammed the door. "He's a lunatic."

"It was queer all right." Archie looked thoughtful. "I wonder what he was talking about. Do you think he might have been tea'd up?"

"No, something else was stewing in that crazy brain of his. There was something shrewd going on that I missed." Fred shook his head as though seeking to rid himself of the nuisance of thought. "He's too whacky. I don't know how to understand him."

Archie strolled to the window, peering into the rectangular shadows that overlay the rooftops. The darkness seemed menacing. He thought of darkness in general, the dark, unexplored places of his own mind. How did he differ in that respect from Giordano? How could he even know how he differed, since those were things inaccessible to him? And what did Giordano mean by his parting remarks? Ravings didn't simply spring from nowhere. Besides, somehow, the painter had evoked something in him. His desire to break out of his rut, wasn't that the stirring, trite as it seemed, of something bigger than himself? The window threw back onto his face a pale reflection of the overhead light so that the planes in which his features were disposed became heightened, giving him a drawn look.

"I'm going to get a little sleep," he heard Fred say.

Archie turned from the window. "Go ahead," he answered absently, his voice sounding separated from him, operating on remote control.

As Fred retreated through the living room and on into the bedroom, Archie opened the closet door and removed a tweed jacket from its hanger. He put it on.

"I think I'll take a stroll before working," he called after his partner. He wasn't sure that Fred had heard him. Nevertheless he went out and descended the three flights to the street. He had a vague hope that he might still run into Giordano somewhere.

Some time later, after having failed to overtake the painter, Archie arrived at the corner of Seventh Avenue and Sheridan Square. For several moments, he had paused to contemplate this stretch of a single block in which the night clubs were wedged together in a row, identical yet varied, like members of the same family. Then, having rejected the alternative of returning home to work, he had proceeded along the street and arrived at the 16 Bar where, shortly afterward, he had witnessed the death of Phil White.

Now on his way home, Archie considered with growing apprehension the likelihood that the cops, in investigating the marijuana angle through an examination of Phil's patrons, would contact Giordano. And Giordano would be quite capable of mentioning that pistol. It had been unutterably stupid of Fred to let the painter see it.

Archie gradually increased his pace as he neared the house. By the time he reached his front door, he had abandoned caution completely and had broken into a run. Once in the hall, he raced to the steps, ascending two at a time.

He was hoping fervently that Fred hadn't decided to go out again. There was a nasty rap for illegal possession of a gun. They would have to talk everything over very carefully.

Chapter 3

It was as though some process, some dynamic of living had been temporarily suspended. The overhead light was still burning in the living room. Two couch pillows lay on the floor. A draft from the open window had scattered some of the Brankowski manuscript Archie had left on the desk. The irresolute atmosphere seemed to invite his intrusion. The resumption of some interrupted labor of the mind depended on his arrival and constituted a kind of welcome. Anxiety could be confronted here. Outside, it could only be endured. So it was a relief to be home. Here, he knew what he was doing.

His first act was to close the window and gather up the scattered pages. Then he proceeded through the open door of the adjoining room. Fred was asleep on the unmade bed. He lay on his back. He hadn't even removed his shoes. A loosened tie was his paltry concession to the custom of disrobing.

There was no repose in that sleeping face. The flat, malleable features seemed withdrawn, turned inward toward the perception of some frenzied and immoderate spectacle in a dimension beyond the waking world and yet not in the world of sleep. The nose, the mouth, and even the soft folds that filled the eye sockets appeared to run over slightly from their originally intended contours like a cake dough containing too much liquid to maintain clearly the form imposed by the mold from which it had been removed.

The lower lip protruded aggressively, forming a kind of small pouring spout on whose tip beads of saliva gathered. Caught and drawn slightly downward by the black knots of his eyebrows, the full forehead had been strained into producing a taut row of tiny vertical wrinkles that pointed like arrows toward that dome of a head whose glazed center sloped into the unruly dark patches of hair that still remained.

The contrast between those two faces, that of Archie bent over that of his sleeping roommate represented opposite poles of character. Between the indetermination of the former and Fred's appearance of truculent affirmation might have been placed the whole range of intermediate types. Yet some indefinable identity linked these two as though each subtly bore the imprint of the same maker. Seen together in their disparity, they appeared to overreach the random relationship of friendship to become joined in some innate brotherhood of sensibility.

"Wake up," Archie said. He shook Fred's shoulder.

The other's underlip drew inward expelling its salivary contents onto his chin. A sigh passed sterterously through his flat insufficient nostrils. Archie's second nudge caused Fred to shift defensively over to one side, his face turning toward the wall.

"Come on." Archie raised his voice and shook Fred again. The other's head swiveled painfully back from the wall toward the source of the disturbance. The closed eyes opened warily and then quickly retreated from the discomfort of the light.

"Huh? What time is it?"

"A little past twelve."

Fred shaded his eyes with his hand, sat up and faced the window, noting the darkness outside. The hand descended to wipe probingly at the wet chin. Simultaneously, his gaze rested on Archie.

"Just get in?"

Archie nodded and sat on the edge of the bed. "Hurry and wake up. I want to talk to you."

"I'm awake. What's the matter?"

"Plenty." Archie plucked out a cigarette, eyed it thoughtfully and thrust it into his mouth. He frowned at the floor and then searched his pockets for a match.

"Well—talk!" Fred said with sudden asperity. "If you've got something to say—tell me."

"Somebody just killed Phil White." Archie avoided looking at Fred who had swung over and placed his feet on the floor. His attention was irrelevantly fixed on his own feet. There was a small stain on one of his shoes that suggested blood but which he knew was only from a fragment of butter.

"What's all this? Who? Where?"

"I don't know. I just came from the 16 Bar where it happened. Right at my feet. I was having a beer. I was finishing it. I was about to go home. Then I feel this hand on my shoulder. It's Phil White, looking weird. I never saw a face with an expression like that on it before. I hope I never see it again as long as I live. Or maybe because there wasn't any expression at all. It was just—" He stopped. It was not deliberate. The sentence was choked off as though some sudden vision had brazenly irrupted within that churned up area of his mind given over to Phil White, obtruding itself so brutally that he hadn't even the breath to continue the hysteric narration that had summarily evoked it.

"Well? What's the matter? What did you stop for?"

Archie stood up, accomplishing in that change of position a kind of escape from the accumulated poison of his thoughts.

"I just can't tell you. There isn't any way of making you understand what it was like. Because no matter how clearly I give you the details, there'd still have to be something left over that couldn't be talked about. And that's the very part that makes me feel the way I do."

"I'll be damned," Fred said. "What a touching outburst of sensibility." He was watching Archie with the wariness of a farmer observing the manipulations of a shell game operator at a country fair. The performance was suspect but variations from the norm were always possible. Archie might be telling the truth but Fred required more assurance than the grotesque recital was able to provide.

"So Phil White's been bumped off. And that's a signal for you to take off on some tragic rapture. A man's only supposed to get that way when a woman leaves him. Look at me. Sylvia stood me up tonight. Note closely the absence of all traces of suffering. Matter of fact, I came home and had two hours' sleep. What was Phil White to you anyway?"

"For one thing," Archie said without looking up, "we aren't exactly unconcerned in it." This was communicated in a voice so muted as to make the interjection of a new element too unobtrusive to be immediately noticed. It was as if Archie, in presenting this new factor, wished first to assure himself of a more favorable reception before committing himself too strongly to its assertion.

A jet of smoke shot from Fred's pursed lips. "Oh—so now it comes. The real story."

"Hasn't it occurred to you that the cops might come here to ask questions about Phil?"

"What if they do?"

"You seem to forget, we've got enough stuff in that top dresser drawer to pull down a nice rap for ourselves."

"You mean the gun?"

"Sure I mean the gun—and the tea too. Only, it's the gun that worries me. You with your great sense of caution—you had to go let that crazy Giordano see the gun. How do we know he isn't going to mention it to the cops when they come asking questions about Phil White?"

"Are you kidding? Is that what's bothering you? You're incredible. You come in here with a piece of news as startling as anything that's ever happened, but you can't even tell me about it straight. All you can do is sit around here and worry about your sins. Somebody killed Phil White and because of that, you're going to be punished for being wicked. What the hell's gotten into you? Can't you give me a normal, intelligible report of what happened?"

"How do I know what happened? He just walked in, started to talk to me, and then all of a sudden he was lying there at my feet, dead."

"Shot?"

"Yeah—shot."

"Well, didn't you hear anything? Somebody must've done it. Didn't anybody notice anything?"

"No, that's what's so crazy about it. Nobody knew how it happened. I thought he was drunk myself. And I didn't want to hang around until the cops came. I wasn't stupid enough to let myself get mixed up in it."

"How would you get mixed up in it?"

"I knew him, didn't I? He was trying to tell me something when he fell." Archie began to pace back and forth before the bed. "Who do we know that could kill a guy, anyway? I've been going crazy trying to figure it out. But all I can think of is maybe racketeers."

"Phil mixed up with racketeers? You ought to stay away from movies. They're making you foolish. What racketeers?"

"What about his tea connection?"

"You're dizzy. He's been getting that stuff from some seaman who hangs around the 16 Bar. I know the guy, a little skinny blond who always wears a sweater. Besides, what makes you think nobody we know could commit a murder?"

Archie crushed out his cigarette in the ash tray on the dresser. "All right, master mind. So who killed Phil White?"

"Well, what's the matter with Giordano? You think that lunatic wasn't serious about wanting to fix Phil this evening? He's done whackier things than murder. Only they're not crimes so you overlook them. Don't forget, Giordano's a totally uninhibited guy. And it requires a far greater absence of inhibition to indulge in some of his caprices than it does to commit murder. Like the time he took a leak in the subway when we were coming back from his one-man show. Matter of fact, I'll bet Giordano did it."

"But Giordano wasn't even around."

"Neither was the murderer, apparently, according to your story. So it fits, doesn't it?"

"Hasn't it occurred to you that the cops might trace Phil's tea connections and come around asking us questions?"

Fred had gotten up and Archie followed him through the living room and into the kitchen, continuing to talk as the other lit the burner under the coffee pot. "And what's to stop your uninhibited friend, Giordano, from blabbing to the cops about that gun we've got? They're sure to get around to him."

Fred turned from the stove, shaking out the match. "You know, I'm really getting worried about you. You sound just like the time we were talking over in Sylvia's apartment about the war and you spotted that telephone lead-in box and drove us all crazy with the idea that G-men had planted a dictaphone in the apartment." He opened the hot water tap and picked two cups from the dirty dishes in the sink. "You want coffee?"

"I'll have some." Archie stood behind Fred, watching him wash the cups. "How the hell did I know? I'd never noticed one of those gadgets before. The stuff you have to bring up. We were all jumpy then because of the draft and the way the war was going. But this is different. We're crazy to keep that gun around."

Chapter 3

Fred shook the excess water off the cups and deposited them on the living-room table. "Stop worrying, will you? You don't know how mad you sound."

Archie sprawled into the overstuffed chair and crossed his legs over an arm. "Well, maybe I am making too much out of it. But I was right in the middle of things. What's mad about getting upset when a guy drops dead practically in your lap?"

Fred returned to the kitchen and came back a moment later with the coffee pot. "I suppose you're too upset to get anything done on the book tonight."

"I'll take a crack at it," Archie said. "After I've had the coffee. I notice that you slept." He stared at Fred's back as Fred filled two cups and lit a cigarette. Then he eased himself from the chair, walked over and sat on the stool facing the table. "I wonder if the morning papers'll have it," he said.

"I slept," said Fred, "because I did my stint on the book this morn—"

He broke off as the telephone rang. They eyed each other.

"For me, probably," Archie said, starting to get up.

Fred waved him off. "Ten to one it's Sylvia. It's got to be her." He started for the phone, calling back over his shoulder to Archie. "She was supposed to call me two hours ago. She'd better make it good."

"Listen—don't let her come over. I've got to work."

Fred picked up the receiver: "Hello? Oh, hello. It's you. What do you mean, I sound mad? How am I supposed to sound? Who were you screwing around with this time when you were supposed to be getting in touch with me two hours ago?"

Sipping his coffee while he listened, Archie pretended to be sorting some pages of the Brankowski manuscript.

"What? Well what about it?" Fred demanded into the telephone. "I know he was killed. What of it? What's that got to do with your not showing up?" He clamped his hand over the mouthpiece and turned to Archie.

"Get this! She's trying to cover herself by asking if I know what happened to Phil White. Acting as if it happened earlier to build up an excuse for being delayed. Oh, is she a strategist!"

Archie put down the manuscript. "Did they find out who did it?"

Fred shook his head. He uncovered the mouthpiece. "Don't give me that. What's the matter? Couldn't you ditch Sydney?"

"That guy Sydney is getting to be a real worry." Archie had joined Fred at the telephone and was standing over him, listening.

"What do you mean, I'm too suspicious?" Fred said into the mouthpiece. "Don't you think I know you by now?" He looked up at Archie, shaking his head slowly from side to side. "Now she says she loves me. That's so I shouldn't beat her ears off." He turned to the phone once more. "Who am I talking to? Archie! Why not? He's right here in the room. I don't have anything to hide. Is that a reason to call me a dirty bastard?" He stretched a hand toward Archie. "Give me my cigarette, will you?"

Archie picked up the cigarette from the ash tray on the table and passed it to him. "Finish up. You'll wear out the telephone."

"Who?" Fred called into the phone. "No, I don't know her. What's she like? Maybe Archie wants to meet her."

Archie was bent over, close to the ear piece, his face touching Fred's cheek. "Has she got a friend with her?"

"Yes. Shall I have them come over. The friend sounds nice."

"Better not," said Archie. "I've got work to do."

"Archie says he has to work," Fred said into the phone.

"But on the other hand," Archie said, approaching the phone again, "maybe I don't have to work."

Chapter 3

"Hold it." Fred called. "Archie's making up his mind."

Archie slapped his fist into his palm. "Am I crazy? Tell them to come on over. You'd think I didn't have enough imagination to think up an excuse for a dope like Brankowski."

Chapter 4

The way in which an event happens to become known can have, for someone like Sylvia Chandler, even more importance than the event itself. Sylvia might have learned of Phil's death through a friend. She might have read of it in the newspapers. Or, as it actually occurred, she might have been passing the 16 Bar at the very moment when the stretcher bearing Phil's body was being carried out to the ambulance and the cover thrown over the still face had slipped away for just that instant sufficiently prolonged to make recognition positive. She was able nevertheless to separate whatever impact that discovery might have made on her from her immediate need to rid herself of her importunate escort and make an already overdue phone call to Fred. She found in the event, apart from its own intense personal significance, the exact pretext that she required.

"I want to go home and be alone for a while," she told Sydney. They had just separated from the crowd that still gathered outside the 16 Bar, watching the police who remained at work after the ambulance had driven away. "I don't feel like going anywhere after seeing that. I'm too upset. Do you mind?"

Sydney, in spite of what he may really have felt, had long ago relinquished his right to such an objection. Having shown toward Sylvia that kind of stoic patience common to certain insecure men, a patience predicated on the hope that its object will somehow alter, he tended through his ineffectualness to increase the demands she made on him. At the same time, he succeeded in attaching her to him by creating in her a growing dependence on his indulgence.

"No," he said. "It's all right."

She took his hand and squeezed it as if, in return for his tolerance, she felt compelled to offer some kind of emotional down-payment. "You're awfully sweet to put up with me."

"Come on," he said. "I'll walk you home."

At her door, three short blocks away, he thrust some bills into her hand. She accepted them mutely.

"I'll see you tomorrow," he said.

"Yes. Good night."

"Good night." He turned away, walking in the direction of the subway and wondering whether he had gained anything by eschewing his usual good-night kiss in a supreme effort to exhibit respect for her upset feelings.

Sylvia waited until Sydney had turned the corner before she crossed the street to the drugstore on the opposite side.

At that moment, a short girl in a green suit, recognizing Sylvia, interrupted her own rapid stride past the drugstore. She paused at a point exactly opposite the plate-glass window from which a small neon sign cast its ruddy reflection on the mirror-like pallor of her face. She waved, lifting her hand in a tight little gesture which was immediately transmuted into a self-conscious thrust of her fingers into the thick web of her hair as though she sought to replace some of that coiled black mass which the violence of her salutation had dislodged.

Sylvia nodded and waved back. "Hi, Dorothy."

She reached the sidewalk and confronted the small sturdy figure who waited with her hands thrust primly into

Chapter 4

the pockets of her severe suit as if seeking through a simulated brazenness to dispel any suggestion of being prissy.

Sylvia urged her friend to join her in a coffee at the fountain. Dorothy was company and, being a woman, represented at this moment disinterest. Moreover the encounter provided a temporary reprieve from the phone call whose painful imminence she suddenly felt the need to defer.

The girls took seats at the empty counter. Dorothy twisted herself into a half-squat on the red leather stool, resting her head on one hand and propping her elbow against the counter. Sylvia's face, half averted, her mouth puckered gravely, was still absentmindedly fixed in that look of suffering which Sydney's departure had now made unnecessary.

"Is something the matter?" Dorothy asked.

"Oh—" Sylvia shook her head, preferring vagueness to a denial of which she herself could not be certain. "Not exactly." To speak directly of anything on her mind involved too much risk in these first moments of meeting. She preferred therefore to question Dorothy.

"Where were you walking in such a hurry?"

"You know me. I'm always in a hurry. Even at a funeral I'd have to hurry. because as soon as I slowed down I'd start to trip all over myself. I wasn't going anywhere. Just bored with sitting around the house. But you—you seem up in the air about something."

"Something nasty just happened. It's no business of mine, but Phil White was just killed over at the 16 Bar. I guess you heard about it."

"Somebody killed? No, I didn't."

"Did you know Phil White?"

"No. The name's familiar though. What happened? A fight? I always knew somebody would get killed in that place."

"No. I just heard about it. But I knew him pretty well once. Which reminds me. I have to make a phone call." She got up. "Have you any plans for tonight?"

"No," Dorothy said. "Nothing special. Why?"

"I don't know yet. I'll see." Sylvia entered the phone booth, ratcheting the door tightly behind her. She dialed Fred's number.

"Hello," she said, recognizing his voice. "I'm sorry about being late." She stared through the glass door at Dorothy still seated before the counter. Then she cupped her hand to the mouthpiece as if fearful of being overheard.

"Listen—don't talk to me that way. I don't find it at all amusing."

His voice jarred back with its blunt presentiment of the truth. But the cynicism of his observation that she'd probably been with Sydney rendered its accuracy irrelevant. Sylvia, in her denial, had scarcely any sense of concocting a lie.

"You're so damned suspicious it's a wonder you can stand being alive. Did you hear that Phil White was killed tonight?"

He already knew about Phil and didn't quite see the connection.

"You're a real skunk," she said. "Is it so unnatural for me to be delayed if someone I know gets killed? Do you think I live by timetable? Can't you understand anything? Fred, who could've killed him? How was it possible?"

His answer compelled her to shut her eyes in sheer frustration. Her lie had been unsuccessful. But the fact that Phil's death really upset her became, through some devious emotional logic, an honest justification for the missed appointment.

"You're too damned suspicious," she retorted. "I won't be talked to that way. Stop it. Besides, I wanted to see you."

After a moment, she demanded furiously: "Who are you talking to? Does everything I say have to become public property, you dirty bastard?"

Chapter 4

It was getting unbearable. She wanted to hang up and run from the phone booth. "Fred, are you busy? I'm coming over. And, by the way, I've a friend with me. Yes, she's nice. Yes!"

Again she closed her eyes. Didn't he understand that she couldn't endure this sort of thing? But obviously he was in no mood to be told about it. So she waited, too hurt even for pride, while he consulted with Archie. She only wanted him to decide quickly so that she could hang up and escape from that phone booth whose walls seemed to be tightening around her.

"Can't your damned roommate make up his mind? Well, we're over at the drugstore. We can be there in about five minutes."

Sylvia hung up. Dorothy had just finished her coffee. "We're going over to Fred's," Sylvia said, joining her at the counter. "His roommate is probably drooling at the thought of meeting you."

Dorothy hesitated. "Don't you want your coffee?"

"No. I don't want it."

"What's his roommate like?"

"Oh, he's harmless if you like it that way. Don't you want to come?"

Dorothy plucked her purse off the counter. "What have I got to lose?" she said. "Let's go."

Chapter 5

The buzzer gave off a series of weak, intermittent rasps like an asthmatic struggling for breath. Fred folded his newspaper and tossed it to the other end of the couch.

"That's Sylvia," he said, getting up. "She always rings as if the button were going to snap her finger off. You'd never suspect she was the timid type. Remind me to teach her to be more aggressive." He stared at Archie who was rushing toward the kitchen with an ash tray in each hand. "What're you doing?"

"Cleaning up."

"What for? You think they'll love you better without your cigarette butts showing?"

"The place doesn't have to be a mess. I don't like it that way myself."

Fred pressed the buzzer that unlocked the downstairs door and stepped into the hall, listening for footsteps on the stairs.

"Hear the thundering herd," he said as Archie returned with the emptied ash trays. "Who invented the myth about women being graceful?"

"They were, back in the eighteenth century," Archie said, setting the ash trays down. "Shall I put out the overhead light? The place looks better with just the lamps on."

"Never mind the scenery. Just pull the shades down."

"How much farther?" came a girl's voice from the stairs.

"One more," Sylvia answered. "Hello, Fred. That you?"

He leaned over the railing and called down. "Your friend has a nice voice."

"Give her a chance to get upstairs. She's almost breathless now."

The two girls reached the landing as Archie emerged and squinted over Fred's shoulder into the poorly lighted corridor.

"This is Fred, Dorothy," Sylvia said. "And that's Archie."

"Hello, Archie said.

Dorothy paused, scrutinizing Fred until Archie remembered to step aside for her to pass. "How's my little jou-jou tonight?" he said to Sylvia. "That's Elizabethan for plaything."

"Not feeling very playful," Sylvia said, following Dorothy into the living room. "That Phil White business keeps turning over in my head."

Fred closed the door. "Can't you wait at least five minutes before turning on the tragedy? Not that I'm really cynical, but I just don't see you going to pieces with such ease."

"He's in his bull mood tonight," Archie said. "Anybody who tries to get sensitive gets sat on. How about a drink?"

"Did one of you do that?" Dorothy was pointing at an unframed painting that hung over the fireplace.

"That's a genuine Giordano," Archie explained. "Like it?"

Dorothy narrowed her eyes at the canvas. "Very much. Who's Giordano?"

"Well, besides being a painter," said Fred, "he's the leading local candidate for the loony bin."

"Why do you say that? What's he like?"

Chapter 5

Archie had placed four jiggers on the bookcase and was pouring rye out of a half-filled bottle.

"He says that about all his friends," Sylvia announced.

"There she goes, getting vulgar. In another minute she'll give you the line about how negative I am."

"Drinks," Archie called. "Come and get it."

"What's so crazy about Giordano? Because he's an abstract painter?"

"No, of course not. I think he's a hell of a good painter," Fred explained. "There isn't anyone around can touch him. That hasn't anything to do with his being nutty."

"Fred has a theory," Archie added, "that Giordano's the guy who bumped off Phil White."

"Giordano!" Sylvia echoed. "Why is that supposed to be funny?"

"He's serious." Archie handed her a drink.

"The trouble with you," Fred stated, "is that you haven't enough imagination to accept the ordinary. Why couldn't it have been Giordano?"

"I don't know. It doesn't make sense. Why Giordano?"

Fred shrugged. "He had reasons."

Dorothy had taken a seat on the couch and was sipping her drink. "If you're so sure, why don't you notify the police?"

"That's complicated," Archie said, sitting alongside of her. "Besides, he doesn't have the right kind of evidence. It's all psychological."

"Besides," Fred added, "why notify the police? I won't miss Phil White."

"Listen to him. Isn't he wicked and anti-social?" Sylvia mocked.

"Me? I regard myself as the only civilized person in the room. The only one with a genuine moral attitude toward murder. All you do is operate by reflex. A guy kills somebody and you automatically run to the police. That's really being anti-social."

As he spoke, he came toward her and took the half-filled jigger from her hand. Turning, he placed it on the bookcase. She watched him, her fingers still curved absently as though oblivious of the missing glass.

"Well?" she asked with a shade of truculence.

He put his hands on her shoulders, pulled her close and kissed her. Her body slackened, then tightened against his.

"Lascivious, aren't they?" Archie said from the couch.

"I hope it's not contagious," Dorothy said. "Can I get some water with my drink? It's too strong to take straight."

Archie got up. "What makes you think it's not? Don't get me wrong. I just smolder longer." He took the glass from her. "Water?"

"Yes. And better get some for yourself before you set fire to something."

"You're a very discouraging girl," said Archie. "Water's in the kitchen. How about keeping me company?"

"All right." Dorothy rose. "Let's fetch water like Jack and Jill."

"Jill gave Jack a tumble," Archie said, leading her by the hand toward the kitchen. "That's just in case you want to stick by the original script."

Fred and Sylvia drew apart. "By the way," Fred asked, "how's Sydney?"

"You're a bastard."

"Why?" Fred shook his head. "I don't understand you. He's a nice guy. He's generous. He's making a decent income. And you treat him like dirt. Where do you expect to get anything better?"

"He's dull," Sylvia exclaimed. "I know he's nice. I like him well enough. But I can't help it. I get bored crazy."

Fred threw up his hands in disgust. "Dull! What the hell are you looking for? It's about time you grew up and learned to accept a little dullness in life. When you were knocking around with Phil White last year, you had plenty of excitement. Is that what you want?"

Chapter 5

"You know damned well what I want."

In feigned astonishment, Fred stabbed a finger at his chest. "Me? Are you mad? What for? To make you miserable? I haven't got a monogamous drop of blood in my veins. I'm absolutely hopeless. When are you going to get smart and stop wasting your time with me?"

"You know I don't believe you."

Fred shrugged. "What's the use. No amount of reason'll make you believe what you don't want to believe." He took her by the hand. "Let's go inside."

"I know you a lot better than you think," she said.

"Sure. I'm not so tough. Just keep telling yourself that. It's all right with me."

They entered the bedroom. Fred quietly closed the door cutting them off from the living room.

"How can two people manage to get a kitchen so filthy," Dorothy said, eying the litter on the floor and the pile of dishes in the sink.

"It's a revolt against early training," Archie said. "We both had domineering mothers."

"Have you two known each other long?"

Archie had turned on the water in the sink and was rinsing a glass. "We went to college together. About ten years ago."

"I thought Fred was quite a bit older."

"Exactly nineteen months. I'm just the perennial youth. Everybody takes me for a kid. Sometimes it's good, sometimes it's a nuisance. Here's your water." He handed her a glass.

She followed him from the kitchen and set the glass down on the bookcase in the living room. "Where'd they disappear?" she asked.

"Retired for the night, it seems." Archie sat down on the couch and pulled Dorothy alongside.

She released her hand. "You don't have to go through all that. I'll let you know if I want anything."

Archie lifted his hands deprecatingly and dropped them on his lap. "You'll have to overlook my clumsiness. Women are so aggressive these days that I'm a little out of practice."

"What? Me, aggressive?"

"Well, I don't know yet. Little by little, I'm training myself not to make snap judgments about women. But do you mind if I make a few experiments?" He tried to kiss her but she pushed him off.

"You know," she said laughing. "You really are a big kid."

"Don't," he said. "You're crushing me. You're really brutal."

"I thought you didn't make snap judgments about women."

"I guess I'm slipping."

He tried to kiss her again and this time she allowed it. But when he attempted to open her lips, she drew back.

"That finishes me," he said. "Your heart wasn't in it."

"It usually takes me a little time."

"I know. You're the duration type. Me, I work strictly by intensity." He pointed to the glass on the bookcase. "You didn't even touch your drink."

"I don't really want it." She looked at her wrist watch. "Matter of fact, it's getting late. I've got to work tomorrow."

"You're not going?" Archie said. Her announcement had had on him the effect of reducing his remark to a mere politeness. He was suddenly out of focus with the smoothly running, untouchable self he had been trying until this moment to project. Like a mechanical toy that had finally unwound, he had ceased to function.

"I really must," Dorothy said, getting up.

"Well—" He sat watching her, bored and no longer solicitous of his desire.

She sensed his letdown and turned in some embarrassment toward the closed door. "I guess Sylvia won't—"

She indicated the door with a motion of the head. "I hate to walk home alone."

"I have to go down for a paper," he said.

"Will you walk me over then?"

He nodded, exonerated from any violation of his code by the happy coincidence of his own errand with her departure.

The deserted street had a faded look in the darkness. They walked slowly and in silence, awkwardly separated, only their hands brushing occasionally as though these extensions independently sought assurance from one another's presence.

"Did you know him well?" Dorothy asked, after they had gone about a block.

"Know who?" Archie said, watching her face which loomed at him from the shadows and became recognizable only by an effort of memory.

"Phil White," she said.

"Oh—" He reflected, in some doubt as to how his relationship with Phil White could be characterized. Odd, he thought, that he hadn't asked it of himself. He was surprised to discover that he couldn't say precisely how well he had known Phil, or even, seen from a certain point of view, whether he had known him at all.

"About three years," he said. "Why?"

"What was he like? It just occurred to me, when someone's murdered, people always think about the kind of person it must take to commit a murder. But Fred was right. I guess almost anyone can kill. So it must work the other way around."

"How do you mean?"

"I was wondering what kind of person it was that gets himself killed. Don't you think that would have something to do with it?"

Archie shrugged and didn't answer.

"Anyway," Dorothy said, "it doesn't matter. It's just a feeling I had."

He was experiencing a queer sense of loss at his failure to understand. She was eluding him, and he couldn't quite explain how it was happening. To be excluded from her realm of feeling was disappointing. He would have liked to bring the same self that had functioned so playfully with her upstairs into line with that more honest self which he felt now walked at her side. He would, consequently, not have to feel ashamed of either.

"I think I do know what you mean," he said finally.

"Do you?"

"Something, anyway," he said, still struggling, not so much to understand as to convince her that he could. "But I don't think I knew Phil well enough to say what he was like in your sense."

"A man has to be very much alive before he can get killed," she said. "That's what surprises everyone. Most of the people we know are hardly alive enough to be murdered."

"I don't know," he said, floundering. "It's complicated." With sudden resentment, he added: "You've got too literary a way of looking at it. Women never seem to recognize the boundary between intuition and nonsense."

"Isn't the sky strange tonight?" she said, ignoring his outburst.

With a forced laugh, he said: "Anyway—I don't feel particularly like discussing Phil White."

"Look," she said, pointing, "those three stars over there. You know what they remind me of?"

Archie was certain now that she was making fun of him. "Take it easy, will you? What're you trying to do— prove you're way ahead of me?"

"Oh, I'm sorry."

"Don't be sorry. Stargazing is a charming occupation. I'm a great admirer of stargazers."

"I didn't mean to make you angry," she said.

He looked at her with irritation. "I wonder if you mean anything. But—forget it."

"But you are angry."

"No, I'm not angry."

"If you are, you don't have to pretend not to be."

"What are you trying to do, make me angry?"

"No, but if it's unpleasant for you to walk me home, I won't mind going on by myself. We're almost there anyhow."

"Well—" He hesitated. "Maybe I'll cut out here."

They had stopped and were facing each other.

"I'd rather you did, if you feel that way."

"How do I know how I feel?" he said sharply.

"Well, who should know?"

He turned suddenly. "All right. You win." Before she could answer, he had begun to stride rapidly in the opposite direction. When he had gone about a hundred paces, he looked back. But by now she was walking on. The sight of her oblivious back heightened his rage, but he lingered to see if she would turn around. A moment later, without looking back, she had disappeared around the corner.

"The hell with her," he told himself. He cut across the street to the newsstand and bought a paper.

Chapter 6

Under the light of a street lamp, he glanced quickly through the news columns but found no mention of the 16 Bar slaying. The absence of any reference to what in Archie's eyes constituted news gave him a distinct feeling of persecution. It was as if his world and consequently his own life had no rating, no status of any kind in that larger area of society whose events figured so prominently in the pages of the press.

With the newspaper folded and tucked neatly under his arm, he returned home with a depressing conviction of insignificance. His distress was not lightened by any recollection of his peculiar and inarticulate failure with Dorothy. And the sight of that closed door leading from the living room and excluding him from the intimacy shared by Fred and Sylvia was the crowning justification of his sense of being severed from everything.

Switching on the lamp, he sprawled on the leather couch, dropping the newspaper beside him, and staring restlessly at the bookcase across the room in an effort to arouse an interest in reading that would cut him off from the bleakness of his present mood.

It was sheer apathy that impelled him instead to reach again for the newspaper. His eyes fell inadvertently on a small item at the lower left of the front page, an item whose heading he scanned without any curiosity.

POLICE IDENTIFY MURDER VICTIM

He had twice passed this in his search for some reference to Phil White's death, never expecting to find it in the anonymous clothing of a headline that seemed scarcely to alter from one dateline to the next. But now the words "16 Bar" leaped into recognition from somewhere in the text.

In Archie's throat there was a painful pressure. He was beginning to choke again as he had earlier that evening. Tightening his grip on the edges of the paper, he bent forward, squinting at the small type with eyes made watery by his feeling of suffocation, and read rapidly. Then he seemed to become paralyzed. His fingers were no longer capable of holding the newspaper which now slipped with a rustling sound to the floor. Only the eyes remained alive in his rigidly set face, darting from where the paper had been to fix directly on the opposite wall where Giordano's unframed painting hung over the fireplace. His immitigable appeared to test the reality of the canvas itself, to question its very existence as if to guarantee the validity of some fearsome thought predicated exclusively on its presence. Finally, he wrenched his vision from its intense contemplation of the canvas and succeeded in overcoming his reluctance to rise.

Taking two steps in the direction of the closed door which had become the monstrous guardian of a realm forbidden to him, he suddenly hesitated. Reflectively, he passed a moist palm over the contrastingly dry skin of his face. Then he turned away as though having decided to assume by himself the responsibility for the step he had wanted Fred's company in taking.

He strode quickly into the dining room and proceeded to the chest of drawers, seized hold of the topmost one and yanked it open. For a long moment, he remained staring at the disordered interior as though to engrave on his mind what his first glance had instantly confirmed. The pistol was gone.

There was no need to rummage further in the drawer. He had known at once on reading that item in the newspaper that it would be gone. A .22 bullet had been found lodged in Phil White's brain, the account had stated, and had briefly reported the police opinion that the victim had been shot some moments prior to his entry into the 16 Bar and had owed his few additional moments of life to the relatively minor shock of the weapon and the peculiar position of the lethal bullet. The police, the item concluded, were seeking the owner of the gun.

Nevertheless, Archie went through the superfluous procedure of sifting through the contents of the drawer, not once but several times. The activity of his hands gave him, at least, an opportunity to consider things. He had to get hold of Fred, yet he was reluctant to intrude on him in the presence of Sylvia. He could, of course, make Fred understand that she must be made to leave. But, somehow, he wished to be able to defer his interruption long enough to allow what had become an almost palpable atmosphere of guilt to dissipate. Something in the very air of the room, he felt, might suggest the awful truth to Sylvia. And this was a secret he dared share with no one but Fred.

There was no question in his mind that Giordano had taken the gun sometime during his visit earlier in the evening. That Giordano had killed Phil White followed inescapably from this certainty.

Closing the drawer carefully, as though it were still necessary to conceal what it once contained, he did a half turn about the room, making an extra effort to avoid scuffing his heels, walking almost on tiptoe as if, now that he had decided against immediately arousing Fred, he had to take special precautions against making any sound that might disturb him. After a moment he was seized by a sudden compulsion to examine the drawer again. Opening it, he repeated his examination. Then, drawn by a new thought, he reentered the living room, picked up the newspaper and reread the disturbing news item. Apparently, up until the moment of publication, the police had no idea of the murderer. Perhaps they would never get Giordano, in which case the ownership of the gun would never become known. Archie tried to let that thought comfort him. But somehow it was a slim hope. He put the paper down, resisting an impulse to clip the item out. He was determined to leave no traces of his interest in the case. It was necessary to be very careful, even to the extent of not leaving newspapers about from which such significant items had been removed.

He crossed the living room to stand under the Giordano painting at which he stared fixedly. He found himself oddly affected by what he saw as if he now understood the painting for the first time. He and Fred had always been vaguely of the opinion that Giordano was a good painter. They had borrowed this canvas from him several months ago, liking it without particular enthusiasm; the satisfaction it gave them had to do with the way it added to the room rather than with any intrinsic merit they saw in the work itself. But now, as Archie recalled some of the remarks Giordano had made earlier in the evening, his references to work, his cryptic statement about being on the verge of something big, he was strongly drawn to the painting, studying it intently as if it explicitly contained what Giordano had only hinted at.

In what way did art lift one out of oneself? What made it greater than life? Death could terminate life. Was death therefore the greater? Water was not greater than fire. No, the thought was absurd. But did not the wild, explosive swirl of the canvas imply the possibility of murder? Archie gradually convinced himself that the painting and the murder of Phil White were related.

He now began to recall what the painter had said about his experience in the psychopathic ward. "If it could happen to me, why couldn't it happen to anybody?" Why, in-

Chapter 6

deed, Archie asked himself. Why, for example, couldn't it happen to himself? If Giordano—a friend, a person who had only recently sat in this room and talked with him, saying things that touched so directly on his own problems—if Giordano could commit a murder, couldn't he, Archie, also commit a murder? Wasn't the murder, in a sense, his murder too?

He remembered the guilty feelings he had had in the bar after the doctor's announcement that Phil had been shot. Even then he must have sensed his own connection with the killing. except that, in that first moment of shock, he couldn't possibly have admitted it to himself.

Finally, Archie tore himself away from the canvas. What circles of obsession his mind moved in. It was all nonsense. Certainly, there was a great deal in the painting. Giordano was really a great painter. Archie hadn't really paid much attention to that before. One never connected greatness, or murder, for that matter, with one's own associates. As for the rest of his ideas, he was naturally upset. There was nothing more than that.

But something compelled him to turn back to the painting again. Suppose Giordano's art really had led him to this murder? What had it accomplished for him? What was Giordano feeling at this moment? What did he look like? What did he eat? Archie felt an insatiable curiosity. He would have given anything to see the painter.

Frightened by his own intensity, he turned once more from the painting. He had to think of himself. He couldn't really accept the fact that art was greater than life. Great painting or not, perhaps it should be gotten rid of. It might be prudent to obliterate all traces of ever having known Giordano. But, of course, that was nonsense. He gazed absently out the window.

With a shock, he noticed that it was already light outside. He had a sudden terrifying sense of the passage of precious time. The investigation might have proceeded very far by now. Perhaps the police already had Giordano. Perhaps they had already learned where he had obtained the gun. They might even be on their way over now.

In an access of terror, Archie moved to the closed door and rapped sharply on it. Then, as there was no response, he began to pound, stopping only when he heard Fred's startled shout from within.

"Who is it? What's the matter?"

"It's me," Archie said, trying to sound calm. He had to remember to keep from Sylvia any intimation of anything seriously wrong. "Come out for a minute. I've got to see you."

Fred answered with irritation. "Can't you save it till later? What's up?"

"Come out and I'll tell you," Archie insisted.

He heard mumbling on the other side of the door as Fred and Sylvia discussed the interruption. He tried to listen but was unable to distinguish a word. Fred finally called: "Can't it wait until morning?"

In exasperation, Archie burst out: "Would I wake you now if it could? What's the matter with you?"

This time he could hear Fred speaking distinctly to Sylvia. "He's crazy. I'll go out and see what he wants."

Archie heard the bed springs strain. Then he stood back as the door opened and Fred, naked, emerged, squinting painfully to dispel the discomfort of his abrupt awakening.

"Well, what is it?"

Archie stepped back and beckoned toward the dining room. "Come on inside."

"What the hell's all the mystery?"

Treading gingerly on his bare feet, Fred followed him into the next room. Once safely inside, Archie turned on him in fury, his voice suppressed to a whisper.

"You goddamned fool! Couldn't you understand I didn't want Sylvia to hear anything? Do you think I'd wake you like that for nothing? Listen—"

Chapter 6

Fred took a seat and looked up at Archie with contempt. "If this is another one of your crazy fits, I'm going to break your head."

"Listen, stupid! Get this! Maybe you won't be so goddamned smug about my fits. You and your impeccable calm—your imperturbable good sense. Do you remember my saying we ought to hide the gun? You said I was mad, remember?"

"And I still say so. Come on—talk! I want to get back to bed."

"All right—listen!"

Archie leaned forward, his face set in malicious anticipation. "The gun's gone—see! It's not in the drawer."

"What? What are you talking about?"

"And what's more," Archie continued, still in the same vein of calculated malice. "Phil White was killed with a twenty-two pistol!"

Fred stared, more bewildered than before as he watched Archie turn away, walk into the other room and pick up the newspaper.

"What is all this?"

Archie flung the paper viciously into his lap. "Here—read it yourself!"

Fred fumbled curiously at the paper, his tone modulated now to the increasing realization that something serious had, indeed, happened. "Read what? Where?"

Archie stood over him and pointed. "Right there. Bottom of the first page. Where it says, Police identify murder victim. Go on, read it."

Fred lowered his head, bringing the paper closer to his eyes. Archie stood over him, sucking intently on a cigarette. After a moment he removed it and flicked a speck of ash to the floor.

"Maybe now you can stir that thick head of yours into a little worrying."

"Shut up! I'm trying to read it," Fred retorted without lifting his eyes.

"Well, that's what I call cooperation."

"Shut up."

"Don't disturb the man," Archie muttered to some imaginary bystander. "He's trying to concentrate." He walked to the door separating them from the living room and closed it gently. When he turned back, Fred had lowered the paper to his knees and was looking at him.

"The gun's gone?" he asked.

"Mice," Archie said. "They came in last night and chewed it up. They must have been very hungry."

Ignoring him, Fred crossed the room, yanked out the drawer and examined it. Finally, he eased it slowly shut.

"So, I was right about Giordano."

Archie was astonished to see him smiling. "Since you're so titillated by your own clairvoyance, maybe you can tell me what we should do now. You don't seem particularly disturbed."

"What's there to be disturbed about?" But the mildness of Fred's tone implied a lack of conviction. It was out of character for him to make such an affirmation without vehemence. Archie perceived this.

"I'm waiting," he said, thrusting his hands into his pockets as though by that act he prepared himself for a long siege of attendance on the other's advice.

Fred pulled a soiled terry-cloth robe from the closet and wrapped it around himself. "Much as I hate doing it, we'll have to call the police right away. Tell them Giordano took the gun and—"

A long suspirated groan issued sarcastically from Archie's throat. "Is that piece of sheer dazzling brilliance the source of your cockiness? To what outbreak of insanity do you attribute your tremendous brainstorm? Jerk! What about us? Do you think the cops will forgive us and pat us on the head and tell us we're nice boys for owning that gun?"

Fred shrugged. "Well," he said weakly, "they might overlook it if we helped them solve the murder. It's happened before."

"Might!" Archie exclaimed. "And suppose they don't? Do you know how much of a rap we're liable to pull down for ourselves?"

Fred sat down again and looked thoughtful. "No," he said.

"I don't know either, but it's plenty." He started toward the small bookcase in the corner.

"What are you going to do now?"

"Maybe it's in the encyclopedia. I'd like to know anyway."

Fred got up in sudden exasperation. "Oh, have I got an idiot for a roommate. Do you have to pick now to become a lawyer?" He thrust a chair violently toward Archie. "Sit down! We've got to talk this thing over."

Archie took the seat, casting as he did so a reluctant glance at the encyclopedia standing in neat rows in the bookcase. "You're the brains of the mob. Got any more suggestions?"

"There's just a possibility," Fred said slowly, "that Giordano didn't do it."

"There always is," Archie admitted. "It's unlikely that he didn't take the gun, but there's a possibility that someone broke in and stole it. It's also unlikely, but less so, if he did take it, that someone got it from him and used it on Phil White. But if he didn't do it, that leaves us even worse off."

"How so?"

"Well, as you said before, if we solve the murder for the cops, they might let us off. But if we can't solve it, our chances are considerably lessened."

Fred struck a fist into his palm. "I've got it. It's the only sensible thing to do. Go over and see Giordano."

"You mean—ask him point-blank if he did it?"

"Why not?"

Archie shrugged. "I don't know. Will you do it?"

"Me? How about both of us?"

"Look," Archie said. "Maybe I'm a coward. But a crazy bastard like Giordano who'd kill a guy over a nine buck swindle—if he feels we know he's the murderer, how do we know he won't take a shot at us?"

"There isn't a chance in a million he'd do anything like that," Fred said. "Besides he probably figures we know anyway."

"Just the same I'm against it. It's too risky."

"We don't have to ask him anything pointblank. We can just drop over and feel him out. Maybe he'll say something and maybe he won't. But it's worth a try."

"That's what you say. That's exactly the sort of thing you can't pull with a guy like Giordano. He may be whacky, but he's shrewd. We practically never visit him and now all of a sudden we drop over right after the murder. Don't you think he'd be wise?"

"You've got a point there," Fred admitted. He pressed his hand in agonized concentration over his forehead. "Christ, why did we ever get that gun in the first place? I knew we'd be bound to get in trouble over it."

"You knew!" Archie exclaimed. "I was the one who was doubtful, if you remember. It was you who wanted it. You called me a natural born worrier and wanted to know what kind of trouble. If it hadn't been for you—"

"All right," Fred said. "Skip it. What difference does it make now? We're in it and we've got to figure a way out."

"I can't figure anything," Archie said. "Maybe all we can do is sit tight and pray. If there was only—"

"Shut up," Fred interrupted. "I'm trying to think."

Archie glanced up toward the closed door. He tapped Fred on the shoulder. "Say, maybe first we ought to get rid of Sylvia," he said in a low tone.

Fred gazed in sudden panic at the door. "Sylvia! I almost forgot about her." He got up. "I'll get rid of her right away."

"Make it fast. And keep your mouth shut. And remember, we haven't got forever."

"Do you have to remind me?" He opened the door.

As Fred went out, Archie lit a cigarette, inhaled, exhaled and stared painfully at the ceiling. He was wondering what would happen if he did actually go and see Giordano. He could never tell Fred that there was some connection between Giordano's art and the murder. Fred would only laugh at him. And probably Fred would be perfectly right.

Chapter 7

It was a small black memo-book about the size of a cigarette package. It had a printed index and simulated grain leather covers which had gotten dog-eared with much handling. Even the gold in the letters that had spelled out the word "Memo" had been almost worn off. It was the kind of notebook easily obtainable at any dime store.

"Some of the names in there are just notes. We can't make anything out of them. But that's where the others might be able to help." Inspector Sheean bit off the end of a cigar and rose from behind the desk. "It should be an easy case. But it really isn't," he told the detective who stood there examining the notebook.

The detective nodded.

Sheean smiled. "Frankly, it's a headache. A routine homicide without any motive. We're sure of that. At least nothing *we'd* call a motive. Some blowtop pulled this, all right. And the Village is full of blowtops. Some of the names in that book we know. Couple of blowtops right there. If Phil White peddled tea, chances are the whole crowd used reefers. The names in there are either customers or friends. It was petty stuff, so most likely customers and friends are the same thing."

The detective slipped the notebook into his pocket. "I'll poke around," he said. "There isn't much pressure on this, is there?"

The inspector shrugged. "It only happened last night. Take a couple of days. Then turn in a report."

"Okay," the detective said. He went out the door.

A few moments later he boarded a bus and took a side seat. From his pocket he extracted the little memo-book. Which of the names listed there should he try first? It didn't really matter where he began but he decided in advance to determine which appeared most interesting. Under the C's he stopped at the name Sylvia Chandler. There were names above and below it, but Sylvia Chandler was inked in heavily. It dominated the page. And beneath the name were several crossed-out addresses. She was young, he decided. The frequent moving attested to that. The last address listed for her was on Bleecker Street. He decided to make that his first stop.

A piece of brown paper had been thrust into the bell plate and the detective had to flash his light to make out the name CHANDLER faintly typed out. He pressed the bell and almost instantly heard the buzzer that released the door catch. Someone, he thought, judging by the rapid response, who evidently enjoyed visitors—unless she happened to be near the buzzer when he rang. He crossed the badly lighted hallway to a steep flight of steps covered by worn gray carpeting. As he mounted, he heard a girl's voice from above: "Hello?"

"Hello," he called back.

"Fred?"

The detective didn't answer, but on reaching the landing, he saw a pale girl with uncombed hair, a deep brown skirt and a plaid blouse. She was standing just outside her open door. Noticing him she drew back. "Oh—" she said, embarrassed. Immediately she added: "Did you ring?"

"Sylvia Chandler?"

"Yes. Who are you?"

He thrust his badge at her. Her eyes fell on it, then lifted quickly to his face.

"May I come in?" he said.

She cast a backward glance into the room as if debating his request. Then she held the door open and preceded him in, her rope-soled shoes making little sound on the bare floor where his own heels resounded distinctly as if to enunciate the authority he represented.

"Won't you sit down?"

For an instant, he gazed at the studio couch whose worn, scuffed cover seemed to proclaim a constant succession of ownership, the deep sag in the center being almost beyond the ability or the possessive instinct of any one individual to effect. But seating himself, he watched her throw a spread over the unmade double divan on the other side of the over-furnished room. She did this with excessive diffidence, so that the effort to mask her anxiety succeeded only in further calling attention to it.

His silent examination finally caused her to stumble over a ridge in the grass rug. She turned to him as she hurriedly pulled tight the corners of the spread. "I'll be with you in a moment."

"It's all right," he said. "Don't rush."

He stared at the summer rug which apparently did more than seasonal duty. Its cleanliness contrasted with the dissociated items of living wantonly strewn over its surface: a rumpled stocking, a pair of black suede shoes lying on their sides, part of a newspaper and a wooden coat hanger. But he saw this untidiness as the reflection of an immediate state of mind rather than any fixed characteristic.

On the opposite wall was a small Miro reproduction in a borderless glass frame. Next to that, in brazen contrast, was a heavily painted oil, its unframed edges jutting sloppily from the stretcher. It compelled his attention long enough for Sylvia to notice it.

"A friend of mine did that," she announced, taking this means of breaking the uncomfortable silence.

He nodded, making a sound in his throat by way of acknowledgment. The need grew in her for eliciting some specific comment from him. She suddenly required his opinion, some avowal of like or dislike. This would at least establish a plane of contact on which she could operate. But his noncommittal response forced her to place his attitude toward painting in that class which she assumed belonged to any cop.

"I don't suppose you care much for abstract painting." She uttered this in a tolerant tone as if she were prepared to make allowance for his being a cop. Seating herself on the edge of the divan, she faced him, clasping her hands in her lap and inclining her head toward him in an attitude of careful attention.

"I'm not prejudiced," he casually remarked.

He took the little memo-book from his pocket and opened it. "There are some things I'm sure you can tell me, Miss Chandler. I don't want to take up more of your time than I can help.

"This isn't about Phil White, is it?"

He smiled. "You don't have anything else on your conscience, do you?"

"I certainly don't have Phil White on my conscience. Why come to me about him?"

"Suppose you let me ask the questions, Miss Chandler."

"But I don't see why—"

"What can you tell me about Phil White?"

"Nothing," she said, "that the law would be interested in. Except that I didn't kill him."

"If you'll just answer my questions directly, we'll save a good deal of time."

"Well?"

He was staring at Sylvia's name and the series of crossed-out addresses in the memo-book. "How intimate were you with Phil White?" he asked without looking up at her.

She hesitated until he was forced to prompt her. "Now look," he said. "My questions might be embarrassing. But this is a murder. I'm not interested in your personal life."

"I saw quite a lot of him at one time. But that was several years ago. In the past year, I've barely been on speaking terms with him."

He consulted the memo-book again. "How long have you been living in this apartment?"

"Only about three months. No—wait. I'd say about four. But—"

Then as recently as four months ago, Phil White felt sufficiently friendly with you to list this address in his book. That doesn't seem to agree with your statement that you were scarcely on speaking terms."

The absurdity of her position caused her to twist her hands in her lap. She felt threatened by her own contradiction, not because she was compromised with the law, but because his triumph over her as a cop was something which didn't fit in with her scheme of things. His triumph over her as a man would not have been at all disturbing.

"Can I help it if Phil White kept my address? How do I know what his reasons were?" Her hand shot out in an angry, emphatic gesture and collided with the ash tray which clattered to the floor, scattering its contents over the rug.

There was a moment of silence in which the violent echo seemed to repeat itself. The eyes of each fixed involuntarily on that jagged circle of strewn ashes, the room itself becoming merely peripheral, magnetized, as it were, by that precipitate core of disorder. Then the detective spoke again, his placid voice disdaining the accident.

"What happened between you and Phil White? Did you quarrel?"

Reluctantly, Sylvia's eyes lifted from the mess and sought his face. "I'm sorry. What did you say?"

"Did you quarrel with Phil White? What made you stop seeing him?"

"No, we didn't quarrel. It was just one of those things. I guess as you grow up you just tend to drift away from certain people." She stood up, holding the ash tray and brushing the remaining ashes over the rug with her foot.

"What about his other friends? I suppose you'd know quite a few."

She sat down again, placing the ash tray beside her. "You can't help but know everybody down here in the Village. Even the ones you don't speak to. That's the way it is—like a small town."

"Or—" he added, "like a goldfish bowl."

"You're not kidding," she said.

"In which case, you should be able to supply quite a bit of information."

She stiffened. "I don't know what information I can give you. I don't know where I come into this anyway. I told you, I've hardly spoken to Phil for—"

He looked up from the memo-book. "Who's Fred Birnley?"

She got up unexpectedly, striding quickly across the room to the bookcase, where, from a pack on the top shelf, she extracted a cigarette.

"What about him?" she demanded.

"You know him?"

"Yes."

"Know him well?"

"Yes, pretty well. I—I do some typing for him once in a while." She lit the cigarette, concentrating on the flare of the match as she added: "He's a writer." She appeared to be waiting for a further explanation as she turned to him. Meeting her look, he smiled stiffly.

"Thanks," he said.

"Thanks? Why, is that all?"

"Is there anything else?"

"I don't know what you mean." She shook out the match impatiently. "Listen, what's he got to do with it?"

"I don't know," the detective said. "His name's here in the address book, just like yours. I'm only trying to establish that all you people know each other." His index finger moved down the page. "This one—Archie Grau—at the same address—are they roommates?"

She nodded. "Yes."

"Who's Steve Cameron?"

"Who?"

He repeated the name. "It's an uptown address."

She shook her head. "I don't know. Never heard of him."

"Joseph Giordano?"

She resumed her seat on the divan. "Everybody knows him. He's a painter. A real character. He used to—"

"Tell me," he said. "Were these people friends of Phil's or just customers?"

"What do you mean?"

A flicker of irritation altered the half-smile, the look of bemused objectivity that had formed his expression for the past few moments. "Don't be naive. You know what I mean. You know that Phil White peddled marijuana. You're all, if I may remind you, in the same goldfish bowl. Or," he added with more menace than humor, "the same kettle of fish."

"Well, what about it? Suppose I do know? Is that a crime too?"

"Were they friends or customers?" he insisted.

"Look, they all knew each other. Practically everyone around hangs out at the 16 Bar. That wouldn't exactly make them friends—or customers."

"You too? That also your hangout?"

"Yes, mine too. Which proves what?"

He brushed the tips of his fingers against his pursed lips. "You must have run into Phil White quite often then."

She glared at him without answering.

"You must have had a hard time not speaking to him," he continued.

"I *didn't* necessarily speak to him." The whiteness showed around the knuckles of her clenched hands. "The place is crowded. Everyone hangs out there. The same faces again and again. According to you, I'd have to spend every evening doing nothing but saying hello to everyone in the place."

"Every evening?"

"Well, pretty often, anyway."

He shook his head. "Must be quite a place," he commented. His voice had an amused off-the-record quality that ruthlessly ignored her increasing anger.

She got up and took a step toward him, thrusting her pale face forward. "Listen—I don't know anything about who killed Phil White. Is that plain?" Her voice rose stridently. "Why do I have to be annoyed with all these damned questions?"

He slipped the memo-book back into his pocket and without looking at her got to his feet. "You're not compelled to answer anything," he said.

"If you'd told me that before—"

"On the other hand," he went on, "we could grab you as a material witness. They ask questions differently downtown. This way, I should think you'd find it a bit more convenient."

His manner mollified her. "I haven't anything to hide."

"Then what's all the fuss about? A man's been killed and it's my job to find out something about it."

"Damn Phil White," she said. "Go ahead and ask your questions."

He resumed his seat and drew out the memo-book once more. "By the way," he said, "did you know that Phil White was killed with a twenty-two pistol?"

"What's the matter?" he asked.

She shook her head. "Nothing!"

Chapter 7

"Know anyone who owned such a pistol?" he asked.

"How would I know?"

"That's what I'm asking you."

"I wouldn't know a twenty-two pistol if I saw one. I don't know anything about guns."

"Who do you know that owns a gun?"

"Well, I did know someone who owned a shotgun. He—"

"I mean a pistol."

"No."

"Sure?"

"Positive. Listen—I don't know a thing. Won't you believe me?"

"Now take it easy." He stood up. "If you're not mixed up in this, nothing's going to happen. And if you've told me the truth, chances are I won't be bothering you again."

She watched him hopefully. "Is that all then?"

He gave her a faint smile. "That's all," he said. "Thanks for co-operating, Miss Chandler." He turned from her and went to the door.

"Relax," he said. Then he went out.

Chapter 8

Sylvia got up, slammed the door and locked it. Reentering the room, she kicked viciously at one of the shoes on the rug. It veered off at an angle and struck the front of the studio couch. She stood there staring at it, yet not actually seeing it, her pale face darkening with the turbulence of her feelings. The pupils of her eyes were dilated and apparently beyond perceiving anything in the room itself. Their function seemed perverted in order that some impalpable spectacle might be observed, something which her entire body must complexly apprehend.

When the departing footsteps were no longer audible, Sylvia emerged from that rapt attitude and stepped backward, seating herself on the couch, not accomplishing this in a single act of release, but as if each particle of her had to be slowly disengaged to prevent damage to the whole. Her eyes found the room again, fixing on the floor, passing bleakly over each misplaced object as if in this accompaniment to reflection she could mitigate the turmoil of her thoughts.

In what light was she to consider now that whimsical, silver-gray toy out of whose short snout death had nonsensically appeared? Was it that same object that had merely been part of a game, a misplaced item in a bureau drawer, something in the category of a joke, displayed to her one evening by Fred who had taken pride merely in having obtained all that at the bargain price of five dollars? It had existed, that gun, hardly worth remembering, as a bauble out of context, an eccentricity on the part of its possessor, like an emerald pin on a lumberjack's scarf. What causal link in the world of emotion could lie between such an object and the murder of Phil White?

Unequipped to delve into whatever impulse of passion had expressed itself so unretractably, she could see only the superficial connections. Fred owned the pistol. Therefore Fred had probably killed Phil White. Not Archie, whose agitation last night suddenly became clear, because she sensed, somehow, that that unfathomable impulse was beyond his ability if not his desire to perform. Fred, alone of the two, was capable of so direct an act. And because she was unable quite to fit in the emotional sequence of Fred's presumed act, fear overcame her. How else might she react to this implication of an unknown element, a threatening and unfamiliar area in one with whom she had been so intimate? This unsuspected suspected threshold in him, whose crossing could promise her only hazards, made him suddenly a stranger. And any further intimate contact with him might evoke that strangeness and plunge her suddenly and without reprieve into its uncharted perils.

She reached for a cigarette from the package on the bookshelf only to find it empty. Turning away, she stared distractedly at the room, wringing her hands in an agony of aimlessness.

Fred had promised to come by some time during the morning. He would be likely to arrive, therefore, at any moment. The fear of seeing him, of facing directly that new thing he had become, continued to grow. She sought one of the butts in the ash tray, straightening the crushed end and smoothing it with rough, incompetent fingers so that it broke apart. She dropped the fragments back into the ash tray and took up another butt.

It was no use. It was like being penned up in an airless closet, waiting, and trying to decide whether to wait or not, not even knowing what she was waiting for and yet needing a certain time of waiting in some neutral place in order to let the various tangled ends come together so that they made some sense. But she had to get out of the house. Where to go? Sydney, perhaps? Sydney who had always been a kind of receptacle for whatever excitements she could not contain by herself, who was the recipient of all the excess that came of trying too much to live and not really living at all. But to speak to Sydney of Fred—to risk overstraining the receptacle's capacity—that was something not thoughtlessly ventured.

She removed her coat from the closet and threw it on the couch. Suppose Sydney were to get angry? Jealous! Would he be capable of actually ending things between them? She entered the bathroom and applied her make-up. Her cigarette burned on the edge of the sink. She couldn't bear parting with that fragmentary solace even for an instant. Leaning close to the mirror, she dusted on the powder. On the other hand, if Sydney chose to break off with her over this, what was his use to her anyhow? It was almost necessary in this moment of need to put even him to the test. Better to be completely without anything than find security in the illusion of his support.

She found herself on the street. It was a warm day and her coat was unnecessary. But the sky was overcast and she decided that it might rain later. Depriving herself of her last excuse to return to the house, she walked in the direction of the subway.

"Say, it's you," Sydney said, opening the door and recognizing her in the hallway. "That's funny. Because I rather felt you'd be over today."

"All right," she said, stepping past him into the apartment. "Don't get telepathic on me."

"How come?" He closed the door and leaned back against it to see her.

She watched him standing there, his face looking dark above the crisp white shirt he habitually wore, a shirt that was always a size too large because he couldn't endure a tight collar, and she wondered what it was he was seeing when he looked at her that way. Then, as he moved away, rolling his thick hips, taking those short measured strides with his feet turned out as if he had already calculated the distance and the proper number of paces to be expended in reaching his object, she turned away, feeling embarrassed and disliking herself for having had to come.

Settling back on his neat bed, she found some consolation in the comfort of the room itself, a comfort that was part of a certain scholarly chaos which actually reflected a basic orderliness. His desk was littered. A blank sheet protruded from the carriage of his portable typewriter.

"Why don't you take your coat off?" he said.

She refused his offer of a cigarette. "I hope I'm not interrupting your work."

He waved deprecatingly at the desk. "Oh, I can let it go for a while. How are you feeling?" He had been preparing a lecture for his students at the university that evening and her interruption was certain to upset his schedule. But his pleasure in seeing her prevented his mentioning anything.

"If I'd felt any worse, I couldn't have made it at all. I had to drag myself here—literally."

"Because of last night?"

"Partly, I suppose. You know me—I always come to you when I feel lousy."

He wanted to acknowledge the compliment but the intrusion of another possible meaning prevented him. He said, "Well—", went to the desk and began to sort some of the papers. "Anything new on the murder?"

Chapter 8

"Must you fuss with that stuff now?"

He turned from the desk, looked at her, then put the papers down and went over and sat in the armchair facing her. "I was just straightening some—"

"You didn't even kiss me when I came in," she said.

He sat up stiffly. "I—well—I felt that last night made you—"

She approached and took him by the chin, tilting his head up toward her. "You're so damned sensitive." She brushed her mouth against his. His fingers tightened at her waist as he tried to pull her down close.

She broke away. "No—No, not now. I didn't come for that. I just meant to be affectionate."

"So did I," he lied, watching her sit on the bed again. "I'm glad you came."

She looked serious. "The police dropped in on me this morning."

"The police? Whatever for?" A swift suspicion crossed his mind. He felt his stomach churn. "About Phil White?"

"Who else?"

He nodded, fighting off the suspicion and trying equally to savor it. "Yes?"

"They found my name in Phil's address book. They're questioning everyone he knew."

He relaxed, feeling ashamed of his fear and a bit foolish. "Oh." His voice became more confident. "I guess that was routine."

"Yes." She tapped her foot uneasily and seemed to be debating a further revelation. He waited, becoming uneasy again.

"Do you know anything about law?" she asked.

"Law? I don't know. It depends. Why?"

"Suppose I know something the police wanted to know, and denied it. Wouldn't that be withholding evidence?"

"Christ—you mean you know the murderer?" He looked frightened in a way peculiar to himself, brushing his soft pink hands over his hair and hunching forward in the chair with his face lowered as if in anticipation of a blow. "Are—are you in any danger?"

"If you'd let me finish," she said.

"I'm sorry."

"The gun that killed Phil White was a twenty-two pistol."

"I know. I read about it."

She asked anxiously. "Was it in the paper?"

"A small item. Just that the police were looking for the owner of the gun."

"That's it," she said.

"What?"

"The gun. If I knew who owned the gun and didn't talk, how serious is it?"

"But do you? Christ—can't you tell me?"

"Answer me—is it serious?"

"How do I know? Of course it's serious." He got up and stood behind his chair, holding onto the back of it with tense fingers. "If you do know, why didn't you tell them? Is it—because it's dangerous? You do know, don't you?"

"Yes," she admitted, after a pause.

"Who, for God's sake?"

She shook her head and remained silent.

He struck his palms heavily on the chair back. "Why is it such a secret? Can't you tell me? Are you afraid?"

"It's not that."

"Then what? What's the big mystery? Is it a friend?"

She nodded. "Yes."

"Oh." He reflected briefly, then inquired in hurt tones. "Don't you trust me?"

She shifted uncomfortably and stared down at her lap. Her voice was low and the words emerged with difficulty as though she couldn't quite bring herself to utter them. "I don't know."

CHAPTER 8

"Sylvia!"

"Well—" She watched his horrified expression melt into one of pain. It angered her. He was acting like a hurt puppy and it didn't become him. He was too amply made, too emphatically formed to get away with it.

"How the hell do I know?"

"But—"

"Maybe you won't approve of my knowing. Maybe you'll think it's better if I tell them. How do I know you won't tell them for me? You're always trying to change my life and my friends . . ."

"Sylvia! Goddamn it!" He sprang at her, his fists clenched and his round, ruddy face showing streaks of white at the corners of his mouth and nostrils.

She eyed him coldly as he stood over her in a clumsy, bearlike crouch, daring him by her manner to make some overt movement beyond that frozen stance.

His voice broke, becoming almost a whimper. His arms sagged to his sides. "Sylvia, how can you possibly—"

He retreated, unable to finish. His face went lax, pouching as the blood retreated too quickly in a sudden transitory preview of middle age.

"Listen," she said. Her eyes pinned him like a specimen to the chair into which he had collapsed. "If you ever breathe a word of this to anyone—" She paused, assuring herself that he was incapable of further reaction. "You know how much it means to me," she finished.

He gave her a nod that appeared to be a sacrifice of his last strength on her altar.

"You remember Fred Birnley?"

His eyes widened. "Fred Birnley? Him? He's the one?"

The pupils rolled in their sockets, revealing the bloodshot, apoplectic whites.

"It's his gun."

He was silent for a bit as though he needed to muster his final energies to respond to whatever effect this revelation had on him. Just outside a car was being started. The whining sound filtered into the room.

"You're not still seeing him, are you?" He might at the same time have been asking permission to pose the question.

"Of course not. That is, I haven't been *seeing* him. Not socially, I mean. But I don't see why I shouldn't do his typing. He pays me."

Sydney's head turned immoderately sideways, then jerked back again, making a complete semicircle in the opposite direction. This was repeated several times as if it were necessary to work off an excess of feeling before he could slow down to the tempo of articulate speech.

"You promised you wouldn't."

"I didn't promise that I wouldn't speak to him. Just because I'm not intimate with him anymore, I can't just sever all relations with him. For what reason? Besides, how can you object to my making some extra money?"

He wrung his hands. "You don't understand."

"I understand perfectly. If there's anything I detest, it's jealousy."

"I'm not jealous. He's bad for you. It's what he represents. A whole environment that's unwholesome. My God, haven't you had enough of the Village? Do you have to get mixed up in a murder too?"

"Who's mixed up in a murder? Are you crazy? Just because some cop asked me questions?"

"But he's a murderer! You just said so. And you're protecting—"

"I didn't say anything of the sort."

"The gun—"

"I only said he owned the gun. That doesn't prove he killed Phil White."

"Please, don't shout." Sydney glanced about nervously. "Why don't you tell the police? If he didn't do it, they'll find out. Why jeopardize yourself for him? What for? What's he

Chapter 8

mean to you? For God's sake, Sylvia. Listen to me for once. It isn't because I'm jealous. I'm worried about you. I—I want to protect you."

"That's what I was afraid of."

"What do you mean?"

"Heaven protect me from your protection. Sydney, if you mention one word about that gun to anyone—"

"Please, Sylvia. Please." He sat beside her on the bed and placed his hands on her shoulders. "Didn't I promise?"

She was silent.

"I at least keep my promises," he added.

"Why you—" She thrust his hands away.

"Sylvia, wait. I didn't mean—" He caught at her shoulders again and in spite of her struggles to break away, forced her to face him.

"Let me go."

"You're going to listen to me," he insisted harshly. His fingers dug in like clamps and held her.

"Let go. You're hurting me." Twisting, she struggled to get free.

"No." With a sudden violent thrust, he hurled her back and pinned her down with his whole weight.

"You goddamned fool," she exclaimed, breathing with difficulty under the pressure of his body.

Releasing her shoulders, he circled his arms tightly about her waist. "Sylvia— Please. I love you."

"Don't." She tried to withdraw the hand that was pulling at her dress.

"I ought to kill you," he muttered.

"You'll tear my dress. Let me up."

"No, goddamn it—no!"

She continued to struggle, but he was too strong for her. After a moment, she lay still, feeling his weight on top of her and looking with wide eyes into his angry, set face.

"You'll be sorry," she said.

"I don't care." He pressed his cheek against hers, burying his nose in the covers. "I've had enough. I don't care what happens."

She tried once more to free herself, but the effort this time was directed not so much against him as in concert with him. Her arms, in seeking to pull him off, fastened about his shoulders and held him. Her eyes closed as he found her lips.

For some time, he realized, he had been listening to the sound of his own breathing and trying to co-ordinate it with hers. But now he became aware of the faint ticking of the alarm clock on the desk. And as his attention fixed on it, the ticking grew in volume until it dominated the sound of his breathing. It made him recall the lecture he still had to prepare for his students and about which he now began to feel anxious. He stirred and rolled over, propping his head on his hand. He saw that Sylvia's eyes were open and watching him.

"Awake?" he whispered.

Her lids flickered in what might have been a response. "How are you?"

She answered with a slow yawn, covering her mouth with her hand and lazily stretching her neck.

He sat up with his back to her and frowned. "It's getting late," he said. Then turning, he tried to fathom the meaning of her withdrawn, vacant gaze. Those expressionlessly watching eyes made him uncomfortable.

"Are you angry?" he asked.

Her lips compressed into a thin line. She sat up and looked over the edge of the bed for her shoes. "What difference would it make now?" she said.

"Well—" He watched as she reached down for the shoes. "I know I acted rather badly."

"I suppose you couldn't help it," she said in the same even tone.

"I don't know," he said, shaking his head. "I hate to be so weak."

She leaned over and began to pull on one of the shoes. "Please. Don't start apologizing. That would be too much."

He slid off the bed and crossed the room for a look at the clock. "I'm not apologizing. I was only wondering whether—"

She started toward the bathroom. "You have some work to do, haven't you?"

"Yes, but—what about you? Are you—"

"Then I'd better be leaving. It must be getting late." She shut the bathroom door.

He stood for a moment, staring irresolutely at the closed door. "You ought to get yourself a good dinner tonight," he called. "I'll give you some money before you go."

He stood in an attitude of listening and heard the water splashing the wash basin.

Chapter 9

Inspector Sheean's coat was draped over the back of his swivel chair. His shirtsleeves were rolled up to the elbow. He had a pencil in his hand which he tapped lightly on the desk to emphasize his remarks.

"Now, what did you say your name was?"

Sydney rested his arms on the chair, watching the pencil as though each stroke had some special significance. "Before we get to that," he said, "I'd like to make my position clear. You see, I'm anxious to help. I don't feel I have any right to withhold what I know, but—"

The pencil came down sharply. "What do you do, mister? I mean, what's your occupation?

"I'm a physicist."

"In science, eh?"

"Yes, I consider myself a scientist."

The pencil tapped softly this time as if in accompaniment to meditation. Sheean studied Sydney. "You know," he said, "police business is funny. A lot of people on the outside get a false impression of it. They think of us as paid bullies —watchdogs. Necessary, perhaps, but not very nice. People shy away from cops. They don't understand us, so they shy away. But the truth is, cops aren't like that. The truth is—" Sheean leaned back in the swivel chair and stared up at the ceiling. He rubbed the pencil thoughtfully against his cheek. "The truth is that police work and science are the same thing. In a way, you see, we're in the same business. Now—" He swung toward Sydney again. With another sharp tap of the pencil, he seemed to be calling his thoughts to order. "You scientists, when you're working on a problem, you like to know what it is you're working with, don't you?"

Sydney clasped his hands and met the other's earnest eyes with obvious reluctance.

"Well?"

"If you want to produce an atomic bomb, you've got to know what the stuff is you're dealing with, don't you?"

Sydney dropped his eyes and made an unintelligible sound of assent.

"All right," said Sheean. "It's the same way with us. When we're working on a problem, we like to know where we are. Now—I don't know you. I don't know anything about you. But there are certain facts you claim to be able to give me. Now, how can I judge the value of those facts without knowing who you are? You understand?"

"I suppose so," Sydney said.

"Then, suppose we get located. Let's see what we're dealing with." The pencil poised over a small white pad. "Now—let's have your name."

"I guess it doesn't make any difference," Sydney said. He would have paid a higher price to terminate his participation in the absurd and embarrassing analogy.

"As scientists," Sheean imperturbably continued, "we're not asking you to commit yourself to anything. This is just so I know who I'm talking to. What's the name, then?"

"Sydney Miller. S-Y-D..."

"Oh—not with an I?" The pencil moved rapidly across the pad. "Physicist? Where do you work, Mr. Miller?"

"I teach physics. I'm an instructor at Columbia University."

The pencil paused. Sheean eyed him with new interest. "Columbia? That's where I'm planning to send my kid when he gets old enough. It's a good school." He drew a couple of lines on the pad and smiled. "Didn't have much of a football team last year, though."

Sydney smiled in weak response. "That's what I heard."

Sheean resumed writing. "Don't go in much for sports, do you, Miller?"

"I don't care much for spectator sports."

"I see. Well, I suppose you fellows have some kind of an argument, at that," Sheean declared. "Ever handle a gun?"

"No."

"You weren't in the army then?"

"No. My work was considered essential."

"Oh, yes. All you physicists were in on that bomb, weren't you?"

"I wouldn't know about that. We were doing pure research. What the government did with the results was something else. Personally, I don't think—"

"Then in a sense, you'd know *something* about guns—apart from handling them, I mean. That is, you probably know all about what makes them work, even though you wouldn't be much good at working one yourself."

"You can put it that way."

Sheean placed the eraser end of the pencil against his lips while he pondered something that seemed to amuse him. "Tell me, doesn't that strike you as strange?"

"What's strange about it? What's one got to do with the other?"

Sheean shrugged and turned to Sydney with a smile. "Oh, something about your attitude reminded me of something I once saw in a Mischa Auer movie. This Greenwich Village artist gets thrown out of his room and moves into the apartment of a friend. First thing he does when he moves in, he throws a vase out through the window—without even bothering to open the window. What's the idea? the friend wants to know. It was ugly, says the artist. I didn't like it. All right, says the friend. But if you had to throw it out, couldn't you at least open the window? Open the window? the artist exclaims. My friend, I'm an artist. Not a mechanic!" Sheean chuckled. "You see what I mean? You and that artist got a lot in common."

"I suppose so, if you want to look at it that way," Sydney said. "But actually, I don't see any real connection."

"If there's no connection, how come all you physicists got so bothered about the bomb?"

"That's something else."

Sheean shrugged. "You really think so, don't you?"

Sydney was at a loss. He opened his mouth to speak, hesitated and then said: "I don't know quite what you mean."

The swivel chair creaked as Sheean leaned back thoughtfully. "Would you know a twenty-two pistol if you saw it, Mr. Miller?"

"No—I—"

"Then you never saw this gun?"

"No. You see, I just happened to be told about it."

"By whom?"

Sydney hesitated. "If you don't mind, I'd rather not mention names. I don't think it's relevant."

An explosive tap of the pencil prefaced Sheean's next remarks. "You see—there you have it. We're both alike in being scientists. But there, the similarity ends. We cops, we're practical scientists. We differ from you pure scientists in one important respect. You like to look at just a part of a thing. That way, you stay pure. You breathe a pretty rarefied air—kind of above the rest of humanity. We practical scientists don't work that way. We've got to see things as a whole. We've got to get ourselves dirty. We've got to stick our noses into all kinds of messes. We'd be a pretty half-assed bunch of cops if we took just a pure interest in crime when our real purpose is to do something about it. That's why, by being practical, as you pure science boys like to call it, we get ourselves soiled all right. But maybe that way we keep a whole lot of the human race from getting soiled. So that's why we've got to have more than a pure statement of the case. We've got to have facts, details, names, places; we've got to see the whole thing. That's why I've got to insist on knowing the source of your information about the gun. I've got to have this person's name. You see what I mean?"

Sydney shrugged. "Well, if it has to be. Of course, we can leave science out of it. As a cop, you have to have the name. All right. What I really meant to ask is that what I'm giving you here doesn't get back. Otherwise, it would be—"

"I understand you perfectly," Sheean said. "You'll be protected. That's what I meant by seeing the thing as a whole. If our policy was to overlook your interests, we'd never get anywhere. Now, who was it who told you about the gun?"

"You're not just promising me all this just to get the information?"

"Absolutely not."

"I've heard so many stories about police methods— but— well, there wouldn't be any point in revealing the source of your information, would there?"

"Look, I know I'm not talking to some ordinary guy off the street. You're a scientist—an intellectual. You should be able to figure that out for yourself. Why should we cut off our nose to spite our face?"

"All right, then. But maybe I ought to give you the whole story right from the beginning."

Sheean stared down at the pad. "You'll notice," he said, "that I'm not even calling in a stenographer. That should make you feel better."

Chapter 10

Fred wrapped his handkerchief around the handle and lifted the pot from the stove. He carried it gingerly to the dining-room table.

"You want some soup? Hey—stupid. Come back to consciousness."

Archie came out of his slouch and pushed his weight back more fully into the armchair. His trouser cuff caught on a loose nail in the chair leg.

"The same canned soup from yesterday?" he asked, as he reached down to detach the cloth from the nail.

Fred picked up a spoon and plucked a slice of bread from the paper-wrapped loaf on the table. He bit off a chunk of the bread.

"It was in the refrigerator. what's wrong?"

"We got to get this chair fixed," Archie mumbled, tugging at his snagged cuff. "What's wrong? How much ptomaine do you need to go blind? Anything above forty degrees can accumulate ptomaine germs in less than twenty minutes.

"All right, all right. You starve. I'll go blind." Fred dipped his spoon into the pot, stirring the steaming contents as he munched on the bread.

"I can go down later and have something outside," Archie said. He stared with disgust as Fred gulped a spoonful of soup. "My God, I can't stand watching you. Can't you use a plate?"

Fred's empty spoon halted in the midst of a descending arc back to the pot. His head turned so that his scornful eyes might fasten on Archie with their total frontal effect.

"How refined you're getting. What's the matter? You don't like peasants anymore? Apparently Phil White's getting knocked off was nothing to you but an opportunity for a sudden, startling display of sensibility. You should be grateful to Giordano. Without the murder, no one would have suspected you of having a soul."

Archie, losing patience, violently ripped his trouser cuff free of the stubborn nail. Then, anxiously feeling the cloth for the extent of the tear, he twisted his head around to glower at Fred.

"Go blame it on my soul because I get tired of living like a pig. We don't have to, you know. We can afford to do it differently."

Fred shrugged. "Frankly, I've given you up. Phil White gets bumped off and instead of employing your intellectual resources, you go in for a kind of conscience purging on the vulgar level of a shop girl. Do you have to start the clean life by working on my table manners? If you want to get rid of your guilt, why not do it rationally? Go ahead and see a psychoanalyst. Be stupid—but do it on a higher level, at least."

Archie stood up, thrusting his hands into his pockets. "And you, I suppose you're so unperturbed about the whole situation that all your irritability is just for practice." He withdrew his hands from his pockets and flung them out in a gesture of despair. "I was only trying to talk to you. I'm still relatively normal."

"Is that all? Seems to me you've been sitting in that chair all day, paralyzed with worry."

"Sure, it's unusual that I should be trying to decide whether we shouldn't go talk to Giordano after all. We can't just do nothing. It seems to me any act right now would be

Chapter 10

better than sitting around here wondering what's going to happen."

Fred thrust the last of the slice of bread into his mouth. "Look who wants to go see Giordano. Why you're so terrified you haven't even got the nerve to go downstairs for something to eat for fear the cops'll grab you the moment you step outdoors."

"You prefer ptomaine, I see."

"You know damned well I'm waiting for a call from Sylvia. I couldn't get her in all day. I've just got a feeling that there's something peculiar going on with her. She wouldn't stand me up twice in a row. Not unless there was a crisis in her life."

"Seems to me there's been a crisis in everybody's life since last night."

Fred swallowed and scooped up another spoonful of soup. "On you, it's not so becoming. Take my advice. Stick to being rational. You haven't got the kind of face that goes with sensibility."

Archie was just turning away when the doorbell rang. He stiffened at the sudden sound. Fred's spoon slipped from his fingers and fell into the pot of soup. They eyed each other.

"Who can that be?" Archie's voice had dropped to a whisper.

Fred reached into the pot for his spoon, laid it on the table and wiped his fingers with his handkerchief. "How should I know? Answer and you'll find out."

Archie frowned, took a hesitant step toward the door, then paused. "It didn't sound like any ring we know. There was something funny about it. It seemed too long."

"All of a sudden everybody we know has a special ring. Of course, I haven't got your sensibility. To me it sounded like an ordinary ring."

"It could be the police. Do you think I should answer? They can't see the light from the front window."

Fred got up and pushed Archie aside. "Tomorrow, I'll play idiot with you." He pressed the buzzer and held it down. "Tonight, I'm not in the mood. If the police want to see us, it won't help to hide under the bed. Besides, I've a pretty good idea it's Sylvia."

He opened the door and leaned out, listening for footsteps on the stairs.

"Sounds like a man to me," Archie said, his head inclined forward just over Fred's shoulder.

"It does sound like a man," Fred admitted.

"They usually come in pairs, don't they?"

"You mean the cops? In the movies—yes."

"Sh—" Archie warned. "Not so loud."

"It sounds like Dave Weiss to me. Didn't he say he might be around?"

The face that appeared above the stair rail was an unfamiliar one. And to the intent, biased vision of Fred and Archie, its objective characteristics were lost. Only one staggering fact was revealed by their acutely specialized intuition. Both understood instantly that their visitor was a detective. So final was their acceptance that, following the visitor's laconic announcement, "My name is Brown," neither thought of questioning the authority of that anonymous identification. Fred held open the door and with an exaggerated inclination of the head, asked the visitor in. His throat had gotten so dry that what had been intended for a firm, assured tone, emerged in a kind of croaking whisper.

"You better not sit on that chair," Archie said. "There's a loose nail. I just caught my pants on it."

Watching as the visitor with a murmured "thanks" looked about for another seat, Archie planted his legs firmly apart without moving from the doorway. It was Fred who, with clumsy, obsequious haste, dragged a chair from the table. "Here, you'll be safer on this." With a suppressed laugh, he pointed at the littered table. "Don't mind the mess. We're just going through our weekly cyclone season."

Chapter 10

Archie carefully closed the door. Facing the newcomer, he tightened his belt and announced: "I'm Grau. He's Birnley. What can we do—or, rather—what exactly is it?"

The visitor watched them for a moment. Fred was distractedly trying to gather together the dirty dishes on the table. Archie leaned against the door nonchalantly swinging the loose end of his belt.

"That's up to you," the visitor declared. "It all depends on how much you'll allow me to do for you. You fellows ever been in trouble with the law?"

"Never," Fred stated firmly.

"Why?" said Archie. "What's wrong?"

The detective drew his badge from his pocket. "No funny stuff. I'm from headquarters, fellows."

"Yes, I know," Fred said quickly.

"How did you know?"

"Well, I—"

"It's complicated," Archie interrupted. "But, we were about to get in touch with the police ourselves. The only reason we waited until now, we didn't want to make any accusations without being sure. Pinning a rap on someone—that's a pretty responsible step."

Fred hastily added: "Yes, we were just talking it over when you came. That's how I figured you for a detective."

The detective held up his hand. "Hold on a minute. Take it slow." He got up and stood between them, looking from one to the other. "Now, what were you going to call the police about?"

Archie excitedly interposed: "But that's why you came, isn't it?"

Placing a hand on Archie's shoulder, the detective admonished: "Now just take it easy. I can only get things one at a time. So you keep quiet like a nice fellow."

"But—"

"Yes," Fred said pointedly. "Let me tell him."

"Now, what were you going to call the police about? And make it simple, will you? Or I'll have you both hauled down to headquarters where they don't like wise guys!"

"We're not trying to be funny, officer. If you'd come a half hour later, we'd have been in touch with the police ourselves."

"About what?"

"Phil White. We know who killed him."

"Jesus Christ," the detective exclaimed. He sat down again and stared at them. "Well, go on."

"We don't exactly know," Archie corrected. "If we knew definitely, we'd have notified the police right away."

Fred turned angrily on his roommate. "Maybe you don't know, but I'm positive."

"All right, all right," Archie settled resignedly into the armchair.

"Would it be too much to ask what it is you're so positive about and your friend there finds so vague?" the detective asked.

Fred hesitated. "Well—"

"Go ahead," Archie said, squirming in the chair. He had once again snagged his trousers on the nail and was making embarrassed efforts to free himself. "We can discuss the academic fine points later. I'm out of it for now. I'm not saying a word."

"Just what I was about to suggest," the detective declared.

"All right," Fred announced, sliding his hands nervously over the sides of his head as he stood with his back to Archie. "A guy by the name of Joseph Giordano killed Phil White." For Archie's benefit, he turned to add truculently: "I can be wrong, but I'd stake almost anything on it."

The detective drew Phil White's little memo-book from his pocket and studied it. "Giordano, the painter?"

Fred looked disturbed. "You've seen him?"

Chapter 10

The detective demanded: "How do you know Giordano killed Phil White?"

"Because of the gun for one thing. Giordano left a twenty-two pistol here. He forgot it when he was visiting us. We put it away in a drawer and he came by just before the murder and took it."

"You mean, Giordano casually left a pistol lying around here and then just as casually came back for it, went out and committed a murder? Is that what you're telling me?"

Archie rose unexpectedly, throwing his hand out in a stabbing gesture of interruption. "You've got to really know this guy Giordano to believe it. He's the craziest bastard around here. I know we should've reported the gun, but—"

"Will you stay out of this?" Fred exclaimed. "I thought you were going to let me talk for once."

"Did Giordano say he planned to kill Phil White?" the detective asked.

"He said he felt like killing him. They had an argument about something. I don't know what it was about."

"We thought it was just talk," Archie said. "Maybe we should have notified the police about the gun right away."

"We didn't think of it," Fred explained. "After you've been around a guy like Giordano for a while, his whacky stunts begin to look normal. You get used to them. In a way, you lose your sense of proportion. I guess that's what happened with us."

The detective regarded them doubtfully.

In a low, petulant voice, Fred exclaimed: "He doesn't believe us. But it's true."

"Every word of it," Archie confirmed. He shook his hands before his face. "I tell you, you've got to know Giordano to believe it."

"This Giordano sounds like quite a character," the detective said. "But as I understand it, the gun is yours."

"Ours?" Fred repeated, taking an involuntary step toward him. "But why?" There was something plaintive about his question as if the shock of the other's disbelief had profoundly saddened him.

Archie shook his head and started toward the door of the adjoining room. "Obviously he's been to see Giordano," he said despairingly. "We're in a spot all right." At the threshold separating the two rooms, he turned suddenly, his hand lunging from his side to circle convulsively over his head. Words rushed from his lips.

"Can't you see it's Giordano's way of covering up—putting the blame on us—knowing that we'd had his gun around here for at least a month—long enough for lots of people to have seen it and assume it to be ours? Oh, what a shrewd article he is! He probably told you he saw the gun here and denied any other knowledge of it. So you'd think—our gun—therefore our murder! But we didn't have anything to do with it. It's not our gun. It's Giordano's! And as sure as I'm standing here, every word we've told you is the truth. For Christ's sake, why don't you believe us? Can't you see we're not criminals?"

The sheer energy of this outburst whose final shrieking cadence was accompanied by a violent movement of the hands to the head seemed to reach beyond the mere possibility of truth or falsehood. Archie stood breathlessly before the detective with his hair ruffled, his watery eyes blinded and his mouth stretched tight across his face like an overstrained rubber band on a bulky package. It appeared that any further stress would burst the very boundaries of personality.

Fred was looking erratically about the room as though trying to recall where he was. Although just as much threatened as his roommate, he was quite incapable of confirming or denying that frenzied explanation which had so far exceeded its own meaning. He was so moved by it that he could scarcely recognize his own real position. Finally, he brought himself to say: "It's all a matter of knowing Giordano. His insides aren't the same as other people's. He's like something from a different species."

Chapter 10

On a sudden impulse, Archie opened the door of the next room and reached around for the wall switch as he motioned to the detective. "Come here, I want to show you something."

The detective went inside, following Archie who stood at the far end pointing to the large unframed canvas over the fireplace.

"That's one of Giordano's," he said. "I thought maybe it would give you an idea. On the other hand, maybe not. Maybe it won't look to you as it does to me. But if it does, you'll understand that it takes a queer twisted kind of mind to paint like that."

"Maybe it does," the detective said, regarding the painting. "I'm not an authority on modern art."

Fred who had followed them into the room stared angrily at Archie. "You're out of your mind. What the hell's the painting got to do with it? This isn't a psychology session."

Archie shrugged. "I just thought—" He turned his back on them to observe the canvas again. He had hoped, somehow, to make clear to the others what he could scarcely make clear to himself, and now he felt he had actually attacked the one thing he should have defended. What right had he to betray Giordano? Wasn't such a betrayal also a betrayal of himself? Could the side of him that aspired to disinterested creation turn on another creative person, an artist in whose talent he now held an unwavering belief? How easy it had been to accuse Giordano without realizing that such an accusation abetted the destruction of his own belief. For if Giordano, the painter, were also a murderer, he, Archie, as accuser must, in effecting the arrest of Giordano, the murderer, also effect the arrest of Giordano the painter—this, despite his own sense of what was not artist in himself, what was merely the commercial writer, being simply the means of guaranteeing his future existence as a creative writer, an artist. He could accept the fact that his being commercial was the means serving his real end of being creative. But now, it appeared, in exposing Giordano, he denied, at the same time, his own creative end. This followed inescapably from denying to Giordano, as artist, the right to immunity as Giordano the murderer. He had confused things impossibly. His reaction had been spontaneous, an act of self-preservation prompted by the shock of the detective's arrival. But was it really an act of self-preservation? What self was he preserving if not the commercial self, since the other self, which Giordano represented, had not yet come into being? Somehow, he would have to make amends. He would have to straighten it all out again. But how?

Completely unnerved, he stood before the painting, blinking rapidly, convinced that it was the work itself that so disturbed him. He turned to Fred and the detective in sudden embarrassment. "Well, maybe I shouldn't have brought it up," he said.

"I don't see that it helps much," the detective admitted, starting back toward the dining room. Fred switched out the light and, together with Archie, followed him.

"Then, what about us? I mean, are we under arrest or what?" Fred asked.

"You fellows have a phone?" the detective queried.

Fred nodded. "Yes. Why?"

"For the time being, I'm going to let things stand as they are. But on one condition. You're not to leave the city under any circumstances. And in case we have to reach you in a hurry, I want one of you here in the house all the time. Is that clear?"

"Sure, you don't have to worry about us."

"If I should call your number and get no answer, I won't waste a second having you both picked up. So don't think you can get away with anything."

"Don't worry. We'll be here," Fred promised.

"Sure, we'll be on tap twenty-four hours a day."

Chapter 10

The detective put his hand on the door knob. "All right, fellows. Remember what I said."

"Sure. So long."

"And meanwhile you might think about getting your stories straight."

He went out, closing the door behind him.

Archie sank into the armchair and pressed his hands to his lowered head. "My God," he exclaimed.

Fred concentrated apathetically on the back of Archie's neck. Standing behind the chair, his hands clenched in his pockets, he reviewed in his mind the scene just ended in the hope of discovering some hint of the real position of things.

"We're in it now," he said bitterly. "Up to our necks. But at least we covered ourselves about the gun. That was an inspiration. Giordano'll have a time proving he got it from us. What do you think?"

"I don't know," Archie said.

"On the whole," Fred continued, "I think we've got a good chance to come out all right." He was silent for a moment. "At least I hope so. But you never can tell."

"I can't understand it," Archie said. "What could've been in Giordano's mind?"

"Maybe he was high. You know how he gets on tea."

"We gave him that stick," Archie said. He raised his head, turning to his partner a face puffed and reddened. His eyes had settled back deeply behind his folded lids giving him an odd infantile look. He seemed withered, like a newborn child. "Our tea, our gun," he pronounced slowly. "Has it ever occurred to you that in a way this is *our* murder?"

Fred shrugged. "That's a weird idea. You seem to be developing a talent for metaphysics. Personally, I can't get touched by the poetry side of it. I'm more interested in saving my skin."

"I keep wondering what made Giordano do it." Archie repeated, speaking as if to himself.

"And that half-witted stunt of showing the painting to that cop," Fred went on. "What the hell did you expect to gain from that? All you did was convince him that you were a little screwy. Didn't you notice how he looked at you?"

Archie rose suddenly from the chair, averting his face as if to keep the other from discovering what was on his mind. "I think I'll go out," he said.

"Now what?" Fred demanded, watching him suspiciously.

Archie made an evasive gesture. "I didn't eat yet," he said. "I have to eat."

"You pick an odd time to develop an appetite."

Archie put on his jacket without answering.

"Remember, while you're out, I have to stay in. That cop said one of us has to be here all the time."

Archie nodded. "I won't be long. He paused at the door to gaze apologetically at Fred.

Fred waved brusquely in his direction. "Go ahead," he said. "Take it easy."

Archie went out.

Chapter 11

He walked slowly in the direction of Fourteenth Street. A cool breeze whirled the dust on the pavement. Bits of paper and torn leaves gyrated suddenly under his feet. A horse-drawn wagon rattled over the cobblestones. He felt exhausted and chilled. He suspected that he was catching cold. But he plodded slowly on, occupied with his thoughts of Giordano. He had a terrible need to see the painter, to look into his face, to get inside the mind that had committed the murder. Until now, he had been unable to bring himself to make the visit. It was almost as if he feared to find out what it was he wished so desperately to know. But the detective's visit, leading him into what he considered a betrayal of Giordano, now made the visit imperative. Somehow, he had to save the painter. He felt convinced that his own fate depended on it.

Giordano the murderer and Giordano the painter were connected. Perhaps, too, they were the same thing—a reaching out beyond life. Murder was an act of supreme arrogance. Its criminality was irrelevant. For crime was only a violation of the mere formal imperatives of legality. And it was not the form that determined the moral nature of the act, not the mere abstract categories of right and wrong, but the content that the form confined. Morality resided in the attitude, the concrete individual nature of the act. Murder itself was an empty word. It described the formal relation between killer and killed. But it excluded what was human in that relationship, the element of feeling, of passion. That was what had impressed him so strongly in Giordano's painting. The formal relations had not been separated from the specific thing that the painting was. The relations became, in short, more than themselves, exceeding mere form, mere idea, mere kind. That was the painting's greatness. That was the achievement that went beyond the mere personality of the painter. And who could question that murder for Giordano was not a similar achievement? But Archie could not be sure. There was something else involved, some link he couldn't find. He shook his head worriedly, kicking at a cardboard box that the breeze had tossed against his foot. He watched it scud into the gutter and heard the hollow sound of its bursting as a speeding car crushed it.

But certainly, he thought, Giordano himself would be able to supply the answer. He simply had to see him, no matter what the risk. There was no other way.

He began to walk more rapidly, turning into the short cut of a narrow side street. It was a gray day, without sun. A monotonous sky gave off a diffused light, creating a shadowless and indifferent afternoon. The chilling breeze came from the river and smelled of dampness. As he hurried on, Archie felt oppressed by something he could not quite place. It was as though some uncomfortable memory had begun to present itself without taking on any tangible form. Yet it was not a memory either. It came from somewhere on the outside. His clothing seemed inadequate against it. He felt naked, unaccountably vulnerable. The muscles of his back grew taut, straining with anticipation. He continued on for a few steps while his sensations crystallized into certainty. The uneasiness of memory had been the face of the detective glimpsed somewhere along his walk. He could not say precisely where. The face had just begun to register. He realized suddenly what it was. He was being followed.

Upon making this discovery, he did not immediately turn his head, but continued walking, mulling over the peculiar circumstance, savoring it as though reflection alone could determine what response he might make to this totally new experience. He fancied that the detective's gaze attached itself to him by an invisible telepathic line so that he became not himself but merely an extension of the other's vision. For in being followed, he had no sense of his being an object of specific interest. It was not he who was in jeopardy. He felt himself functioning merely as a means. It was through him that the detective expected to be led to something else. Otherwise it would be unnecessary to follow him. The detective could simply arrest him.

This idea had for Archie a perverse fascination. He was loath, therefore, to turn around and seek out his wary pursuer, fearing by such an act to break the spell of his fancy. For the detective, in following him, magically conferred on him his own inquisitiveness, so that he became, by identification, a detective.

This feeling gave him, somehow, the right to spy on Giordano, made it, in fact, official. He acquired a certain authority, so that the things he needed to discover about the painter were now properly his to know. He was no longer a mere petitioner of Giordano's, but his equal. It was a relationship of detective versus criminal, not Archie versus Giordano. This reduction of the experience to abstract terms freed him from the burden of his own personality. His right to enter Giordano's studio was established through the circumstance that in representing the law, his personal, individual relation to the world and to Giordano was canceled out.

In such an equation, moreover, the detective and the criminal, in being equal, became the same. He recalled some remarks Fred had made several months ago about certain young hoodlums in the neighborhood, declaring that if they didn't grow up to become criminals, they would become policemen. And it was true that the pure thief and the pure detective were equally devoted to authority, the former to fight it, the latter to uphold it. And both were therefore, outside of life, dedicated, each in his own way, to the principle of order, like monks wedded to an absolute law, to God, to a selflessness that eschewed any of the personal problems of belonging to the world. His quest became, consequently, in the sense of Giordano's remarks about art, something beyond life, a search for truth that transcended his personal fears. This idea, in spite of its haziness, gave Archie a moment of exaltation. He was convinced that he stood on the verge of some vast insight. Momentarily, he expected to be transformed.

The street floor of the Fourteenth Street loft building where Giordano had his studio was occupied by a cafeteria. The entrance to the building lay just a few feet beyond the cafeteria's revolving door. Having arrived, Archie paused and, prompted by an obscure impulse, pushed his way into the cafeteria.

He lingered for a confused moment under the ocherous neon glare, then mechanically drew a check from the turnstile at the entrance and continued on toward the steam table. He stopped at the coffee counter and passed the back of his hand across his forehead. Wonderingly, he stared at the moisture that his knuckles had gathered up. He had not until this moment been aware of his disturbed state. But the strain now became noticeable throughout his body, manifesting itself in a sustained quivering similar to what he had often experienced after a period of intense exertion.

He lifted his face to the chrome dial of the clock above the coffee urns, then without moving his head, shifted his gaze furtively toward the revolving door by which he had entered. If the detective had followed him in, he might already have taken a seat. The place was fairly crowded. Most of the tables were occupied. He turned now to observe with suspicion a man who sat alone near the window, his face and upper body, except for his arms, hidden behind the façade of an open newspaper. From where he stood, it was impossible to get a view of the man's face. Yet the sensation of being still under surveillance possessed him.

He picked up a cup of coffee poured by the counterman and held out his check to be punched, concentrating on the movements of the man's hands as he notched the proper figure on the pasteboard stub and then dropped it into Archie's saucer so that it lay half-immersed in a pool of coffee that had trickled over the cup's edge.

He threaded his way cautiously among the tables and found a vacant seat along the wall opposite the steam table from which point he could observe, across a span of several yards, those mysterious opaque columns of print which seemed somehow more threatening than the face they presumably hid. Once seated, Archie felt a diminution of his nervous reactions. His weight was diffused in the solidity of the chair. The quivering lessened and his body felt organized again. He sipped his coffee, peering over the cup's rim toward the man at the window.

The abrupt change in his plan to see Giordano had occurred, he now tried to tell himself, out of a sheer physical refusal to climb the long flights to the studio. His fear had sucked the strength from his limbs, although he had not at the moment of decision been aware of the existence of his fear. Now that the spell had been broken, he could grasp the whole thing. His fantasy about being a detective had given him a chance to get away from himself, to escape his panic by becoming something else. Could that have been the solution that Giordano had arrived at in the psychopathic ward when he had learned to surpass his personal misery? Because if it was, Archie knew now, it was all wrong. No, something else was involved, something that he hadn't yet grasped. Giordano, perhaps, could tell him. Or perhaps the whole thing was part of a growing obsession. He didn't know. He could scarcely think any more.

Perhaps it was not at all because he was too shaken to climb those stairs that he had avoided Giordano, but because, in the final analysis, he hadn't been sure of how he was connected with the crime. Because he still felt a responsibility for the murder! It had been his gun, after all. And so, he too was the criminal. And the detective was pitted against *him*. So he had turned aside at the last moment out of uncertainty, to spy, not on Giordano, but on the detective. Wasn't he, in fact, spying on the detective at this very moment?

He lowered the cup and gazed down at the table. His head ached with confusion. It was getting unbearable. He would have to break the impasse somehow. Whatever came of it would be better than the kind of torture he was now enduring.

He pushed back his chair, rose from the table, and began walking intently toward the man at the window. It seemed that the distance was taking an interminable time to cover. Then a new thought projected itself. He suddenly realized that there was one other possibility confronting him that might perhaps be worse than his present uncertainty. It had not occurred to him until this moment. But so much had been employed in gathering himself for this move that, like a modern army on the march whose momentum can no longer be countermanded by a mere order, it was impossible to check himself. He strolled up past the table, past the screen of the newspaper and gazed directly at the man behind it. His latest fear was fully confirmed. The solitary occupant of the table was not the detective.

Without stopping, Archie veered away and continued toward the cashier's desk. He paid his check and, pushing his way to the street, set out rapidly in the direction of home. He was convinced now that he had not been followed at all. But he needn't necessarily conclude that his mind was behaving peculiarly. His suspicion, under the circumstances, had really been perfectly normal.

Chapter 12

The detective, after leaving Archie and Fred, had gone directly to Fourteenth Street. Entering the tiled hallway of the loft building where Giordano lived, he discovered on the wall just past the wrought-iron cage of the elevator, a white cardboard sign with the name GIORDANO lettered in black india ink. An arrow pointed diagonally up the staircase at the end of the vestibule.

He climbed three flights of stairs and stood for a moment outside the old-fashioned, gray-painted door on which was pinned a small card with GIORDANO written out in longhand. The transom overhead was open. He could hear the sound of someone walking about inside.

He knocked. The footsteps ceased for an instant, then grew louder as they approached the door. A lock rattled on the other side. Giordano stared out at his visitor through pale eyes that contrasted oddly with the gloss of his tightly combed and parted black hair.

"What do you want?" Giordano's delicate voice contained no inflection other than what was necessary for the bare query.

The detective displayed his badge. Giordano's thin eyebrows went up. He smiled and it seemed that the smile was also a badge, as if Giordano were countering the legal credentials of authority with his own, namely, his right to be what he was, to feel what he felt, and to show, if he chose, a detached interest in the visitor that had nothing to do with any threat to himself.

"You're a detective," Giordano said, as though the novelty of the fact delighted him. "Come in."

He stepped back and, as the detective entered, watched him with close attention as a child might gaze at some newly discovered object, not concerned with its presence so much as the curious fact of its existence.

Giordano's studio had a high ceiling and two large windows that let in a steady flow of light which the flat-white walls distributed evenly. On a large square of linoleum spread in the center of the bare, splintered floor boards stood an empty paint-spattered easel. A table next to the easel supported a glass palette of unusual size. Against the far wall rose a series of wooden racks constructed of packing crates. These contained an assortment of canvases. A cot rested between the windows and a red leather armchair next to the cot seemed like an anomalous luxury in the monk-like, orderly workshop. The unadorned walls and the absence of a single canvas that one might look at gave a peculiarly conspiratorial air to the place as if what work was done there was of such intense private concern as to exclude any casual observer.

"That murder stirred things up around here. Imagine me getting a visit from a detective." Giordano was standing near the door, measuring tobacco from an oilskin pouch into a small blackened pipe. "You don't look much like a detective. But I imagine no one ever really does. What're you going to do when you catch the murderer—hang him or electrocute him?"

The detective seated himself on the edge of the cot. "Do you make your living at painting?" he asked.

Giordano put the pipe in his mouth and walked over to peer at the surface of his palette. "That's a good question. But wait a minute," he said, "until I find a match. You know

Chapter 12

why I like that question? Because it's such a peculiar one. It confuses me. I don't know whether you're a detective interested in an artist's problems or whether art is just a way of getting at something else." He stood over the palette and looked distractedly around. "Now where in hell did I put those matches?"

The detective drew matches from his pocket, struck one and held the light. Giordano, however, took the burning match from his hand and applied it himself, puffing quantities of smoke into the air.

"Thanks," he said.

"I saw one of your paintings this afternoon," the detective continued. "At the house of a couple of friends of yours."

Sinking into the leather chair, Giordano nodded. "I can see this is going to be nice and sociable. So, you saw my painting. Well, I've been struggling with painting for about twelve years. It's too bad you couldn't appreciate it."

"You're quite a wise guy," the detective said.

"Maybe so. You know why?" Giordano narrowed his eyes confidentially. "Because you come in here and start to talk about my painting." He paused. "All right! A detective who talks about my painting is a cagey guy. You want to find out if I murdered Phil White. So what does it mean, your talk about painting? You couldn't be interested in painting. Not as long as you're a detective. In short—" Giordano rose and described a horizontal semi-circle with his pipe. "In short, why not drop the crap? What is it you really want to know?"

"You really are a wise guy," the detective said.

"That's the second time you mentioned it," Giordano replied. "You're a typical detective all right. I used to hang out in the mornings at Jefferson Market Court to watch the comedy. I saw lots of detectives around. You've got the same kind of stamped-out look, now that I observe you closely.

Maybe several years back you could have been something else. But there's no trace left of it now."

"Okay, Giordano," the detective said. "If you want to horse around, that's your business. Because if you don't answer my questions here, you'll only have to do it at the station, so why make it harder on yourself? I've been on this job a long time—seven years. And I've seen enough guys like—"

"Seven years? That's a long time. That's enough to ruin you completely. It doesn't even pay for me to talk to you like a human being any more."

"A comedian too," the detective commented. "Okay. I was only trying to treat you like a regular guy. I've got nothing against you—not yet. Why were you so sure I wasn't just interested in painting? What makes you think I have to have something up my sleeve? Cops are people too."

"Ah," Giordano exclaimed. "Interested! That's different. That's not *liking* painting. If something interests you, it's a problem. For all I know, you may hate painting. Because it's so far out of your world, it has to worry you. Being a detective for seven years, you probably do hate painting."

The detective got to his feet. "Let me know when you're through clowning," he said. "I guess you know that nobody can make you answer my questions. That's up to you. But when you're ready, suppose you tell me about that twenty-two pistol."

"I like you better that way," Giordano said, puffing on his pipe while he watched the detective with amused detachment. "Without trimmings. But your question's a tough one. A twenty-two pistol is a very complex thing. It would take me hours to figure how such a thing rated in my experience. I'm no good at philosophy."

"Where's the pistol, Giordano?"

"I take it you don't mean the pistol in the Platonic sense. You seem to mean a very definite pistol."

Chapter 12

The detective shrugged. "If that's how you feel about it, it's all right with me. Later on, it won't be so funny." He started toward the door. "With the stuff we've got on you now, you're going to sweat, boy. I was only trying to make it easier."

Giordano gestured with his pipe. "That's all right," he said. "If it'll make you feel any better, I won't mind it as much as you think. Why don't you arrest me now? Maybe that'll help."

"I'll arrest you when I'm ready," the detective announced, suddenly angry.

"Wait a minute," Giordano said, seeing that the man was about to leave. "If you've got all that stuff on me, as you say, you must be convinced I'm the murderer. And if you are—well—what are you waiting for?"

"What makes you hint you're the murderer?" the detective asked. He stood in the open doorway and regarded the painter slyly.

Giordano made a movement with his shoulders. "Am I allowed to be subtle?"

"What's on your mind?"

"I mean—in the presence of a detective—which is the only part of you I recognize—can I be subtle in a way that had nothing to do with detectives?"

"I'm willing to listen to anything you have to say to me, Giordano."

"Why do I hint I'm the murderer? You want to know? I'll tell you. Because you showed an interest in my painting. Maybe I'm a murderer in the same way that you're interested in painting."

The detective shook his head in disgust. "Answer me one thing. Haven't I been civil with you?"

"Civil? I'm not so sure. You know what's bothering me?" Giordano took the pipe from his mouth, holding it by the bowl as he jabbed the stem at the detective. "Guys like you make me realize—" Giordano looked very serious "—

what a wonderful world it really is. You know that? It's a fine world. The only trouble is, everybody's full of crap." He thrust the pipe back between his teeth and began sucking on it.

"I give up," the detective said, stepping into the hall. He turned back for a moment to announce in a tone that was neither rage nor discomfort but a confusion of both. "You'll be hearing from me again—soon." Then he slammed the door.

Chapter 13

Sydney had decided after his visit to police headquarters that he would give himself a week before going to see Sylvia again. He counted on this inordinate lapse of time to establish a number of things in his favor. First, it would mitigate the bad impression he had made when she had last visited him and even create in her a certain anxiety over his unaccountable failure to get in touch with her. Second, it would allow sufficient time for the mechanism of the law to involve Fred so that by the end of the week, Sylvia's situation would have altered in the direction of an increasing dependence on himself. Finally, there was the mere factor of the lapse of time whose effect couldn't really be predicted but which would be likely to have some influence on a relationship in which, Sydney had begun to feel, any change would be a relief.

For the first two days, Sydney had had no difficulty in carrying out his plan. The passing of each of those twenty-four hour periods had been observed by him with gloating satisfaction. He regarded himself as having scored a personal triumph over Sylvia as well as a moral triumph over himself in not having succumbed to his feelings and rushed directly to see her.

On the morning of this, the third day, however, he began to experience the first real weakening of his resolve. He had risen several hours later than was habitual with him and, while he had no classes on this day, he planned to finish some research he had undertaken some time ago. Instead, he spent the first part of his day minutely scanning the newspapers for further accounts of the Phil White case and, having discovered nothing, found himself reduced to speculating on the possible effects of the information he had supplied the police.

It seemed reasonable to suppose that Fred had been taken into custody, unless, and this was something that occurred to Sydney only now, the information Sylvia had given him had been incomplete. Suppose, for example, she were more deeply involved than she had admitted. Suppose, for any number of reasons, she had actually lied to him. He knew that she could lie to him easily, knowing this almost out of his own need for lying to her. Then, since he knew little of police methods, at times attributing to them an efficiency that surpassed all credibility and at other times an absurd ineptitude, he began to wonder whether, in checking on the truth of Sylvia's story, they hadn't unearthed some facts that revealed her own culpability.

Why, for example, had Sylvia been so reticent in revealing her knowledge of the gun's ownership? If Fred no longer meant anything to her, as she insisted, it would not be necessary to protect Fred from Sydney. Perhaps in order to divert his insistence from uncovering her own guilt, she had completely fabricated Fred's ownership of the pistol. In that case, it would be Sylvia and not Fred whom the police would be investigating. By the time the week had elapsed, Sylvia might have been caught irretrievably in the meshes of the law and rather than his having gained anything by the time, he could actually have lost the chance of aiding her through a crisis whose rarity might exclude his ever again having such an opportunity. In short, life had proffered a leading role in a romantic drama and by stubbornly adhering to his plan and remaining in ignorance of the situation, he was allowing it to slip by.

Chapter 13

There were alternate possibilities that suggested themselves. Suppose Sylvia had not lied to him. Then it could be assumed that her desire to protect Fred was out of a stronger interest in him than she had been willing to profess. Originally, that had been Sydney's suspicion. But the conclusion that was now forced upon him differed considerably from the earlier one.

Fred's peril might have so wholly engaged Sylvia's attention as to completely banish Sydney from her thoughts. He had been naive in reasoning that by going to the police he would be getting Fred out of the way and leaving a clearer field for himself. Quite the contrary! The longer he kept himself from seeing Sylvia, the greater was the danger of losing her. Two crucial days had already passed. How could he risk a third day?

Greatly disturbed, he decided that he couldn't afford to let another hour pass without taking some definite step. In order to do that, however, he had to have information.

He got up from the armchair in which he had been conducting his speculations and examined himself in the mirror. He'd originally put on the shirt he'd worn the day before in anticipation of a day of work. It was rather soiled. He would have to change it. It wouldn't do to appear before the police inspector in a soiled shirt. Not if he wanted to separate himself in the latter's eyes from the Village.

From the dresser, he extracted a clean white shirt. He stripped off the old one and tossed it on the bed. He was in too much of a hurry to put it in the hamper, despite his rigid practice of never leaving his clothes lying about.

Shortly after, he was on the street, walking rapidly in the direction of the subway. Perhaps the inspector wouldn't tell him whether Fred had been arrested in connection with the gun. Besides, it wouldn't be easy to ask directly for the information. He'd have to phrase his questions obliquely, as if he were less concerned with the people involved than in the triumph of justice. He would appear simply as a citizen who felt a responsibility about an affair in which he'd been inadvertently involved. That was the best approach.

The subway kiosk was on the next corner. Sydney reduced his stride, feeling the necessity of having everything set in his mind before committing himself to the train that would bring him to Sheean's office. It had suddenly begun to strike him that framing the actual concrete questions was going to be difficult. He started to suffer twinges of embarrassment as he projected himself into the interview.

He now recalled how the inspector had forced him into giving his name and Sylvia's at the previous interview. And then there was all that nonsense about police business being science. It had been quite a torture. What was more, the inspector hadn't been particularly friendly. He hadn't chatted about the case with him, sharing what he knew with Sydney, who, as a civic-minded person performing his stern duty, certainly had earned the right to be taken into confidence. At least, the inspector might have treated him more as an equal.

Arriving at the subway entrance, he dallied on the corner, by this time reluctant to go on and yet not certain, since he felt the need for action, what else he might do. Finally, without having made up his mind, he descended the steps and gained the subway platform.

A few moments later, he boarded a train. But he knew that, while he'd be getting off at Fourteenth Street, it wouldn't be to see Sheean. It was as if, having made this decision, he had known all along that he was going to see Sylvia.

She was in the midst of housecleaning when he entered. Most of the apartment's smaller furnishings were piled on the double bed. The rug had been rolled up and placed in a corner. In the center of the floor stood a bucket of gray, soapy water.

The far end of the room had already been mopped. It was still wet. Sylvia, about to begin on the forward half, stood holding the mop and looking distractedly at Sydney as he entered.

Her hair had been pinned up. A film of perspiration made her face gleam. She was wearing a soiled plaid shirt and a long dirndl that was torn down one side, revealing her thigh and hanging voluminously over her bare white legs. A pair of sandals provided protection for her already wet and dirty feet.

"Housecleaning, I see." Sydney said it with relish as if by emphasizing the obvious, he could make it comic.

"You're getting more observant every day. Watch out. Don't step on the wet parts," she said.

He looked about, momentarily disconcerted at not finding a place to sit. Finally, he shifted some of the things on the bed and made a small place for himself. "Don't ask me to sit down," he said, astonishing himself with what he considered his own airiness. "I can help myself."

"This damned floor—it's so old, it's impossible to clean. Don't you have classes today?"

He sat down and watched her with a sly, mocking smile. "You make a good Cinderella."

She started to slosh the mop over the floor again.

"Pick up your feet," she said. "I've got to get under there."

He refused to be dismayed by her lack of attention. He was suddenly feeling too sure of himself. The smile had gotten fixed on his features as though he had overlooked it. "What brought all this on?" he asked, lifting his feet so she could run the mop past the bed. "You look good with a mop. It delights me to behold such a strong domestic streak in you."

She leaned on the mop and eyed him. "What the hell are you babbling about?"

But he was too far launched in his mood to be stopped. He waved offhandedly at her. "Don't let it bother you. Consider me a curious bystander. An inside sidewalk superintendent. I like watching you clean house."

She was clearly puzzled by his manner. It was as if he had something on her. It disturbed her. "Since I didn't issue announcements of my intention to clean house, I don't imagine you came here just to watch me," she said, attempting to prod him with a display of nastiness.

"No," he said, admitting her charge with a modest air. "I did have other reasons for coming."

He felt so secure in his present mood, so firmly protected by it that he was prepared to say anything. He felt himself to be in a condition of rare omnipotence. Consequently, he was able to add in a tone of genuine casualness: "How about Fred? Have the cops grabbed him yet?"

"I haven't seen him," she retorted,

"Why? Has he got someone else to do his typing?"

She glared at him and pushed the mop furiously across the floor.

Sydney considered the increased domestic zeal she displayed and took it, along with her silence, as a good sign. He was doing very well, he decided. He was doing so well that it would be stupid to waste his opportunity. But in what way could he make the most of it?

A reckless thought entered his mind. He even startled himself at the audacity of it. Yet, somehow, the more he considered it, the more he was tempted. It would be a kind of test, a trial of strength. He would do it. He would risk it. Besides, what had he to lose when all was said and done?

"You know—" he began, and then abruptly stopped, overcome by his own contemplated temerity.

Sylvia faced him curiously in the midst of wielding the mop. "What did you say?"

He experienced a kind of heart spasm. He felt a trifle out of breath. But he overrode his momentary impulse of caution and forced himself to proceed. "You know," he repeated. "I'm rather surprised we haven't heard anything yet."

"What do you mean?"

Chapter 13

"About Fred."

She ceased mopping and looked truculently at him. "What about Fred?"

If he faltered now, everything was lost. He had to sustain the mood. The mood would get him through. He compelled himself to go on.

"About Fred being arrested," he said.

"Why should he be arrested?"

"The gun! Because of the gun! Why else?"

"What makes you think the cops know about the gun?"

It was not too late to back down now. He could still shrug it off.

"Because I told them!" The words were out of his mouth before any alternative decision could check them. He was terrified at what he had done, but he kept his face fixed on hers and the smile was still there, a barrier against her recriminations. He even observed with what calmness of demeanor he confronted her, noting at the same time with surprise the very definite paleness that settled on her countenance. He had to tell himself that the alteration of her normal pinkish color was a startling thing to watch. He appended the further assurance that there was nothing she could do to him.

"You told them what?" she asked. "Who's them?" She was positive after the first shock that he had meant something other than what she had understood.

"Why—the police, of course." He allowed the smile to dissolve into an expression of indifference. There wasn't any way he could be stopped now, he realized. He could get away with anything, absolutely anything. "I told the police about Fred being the owner of the gun."

She remained staring at him, appearing less shocked than incredulous, curious rather than angry, trying to act as if he were lying because she couldn't allow herself to admit that she knew he was telling the truth. Her hands clung to the upright pole of the mop. Her weight bore down on it, forcing a trickle of water from the sodden strands. "What kind of a joke is that supposed to be?" she asked.

He wagged his head unconcernedly, safe in the knowledge that she knew he wasn't joking. His excitement was so great that he even wanted to wink at her. It took considerable effort to restrain himself.

"All right," he said. "It's a joke. Let it go at that."

She seized on his remark, deliberately misinterpreting it, finding in it a sudden hope. "You mean—it's a joke?"

"No, it's the truth."

"You told the police?"

He nodded. "I told them as much as I knew. I'm surprised they haven't come to see you to verify the story. Or maybe they did."

She shook her head. "No," she said, too amazed to recognize her own position and responding to his direct question with a childlike lack of continuity.

"Then they must have gone directly to Fred," he went on, disguising his exhilaration with affability. "But on the other hand, wouldn't we have heard if he'd been arrested? What do you think?"

She dropped the mop and moved closer to him, looking anxiously into his face.

"You did," she said. "You really went to the police. I believe you. I honestly do. But how? What for? Don't you realize what a terrible thing—a crazy thing—Sydney, what in hell is wrong with you? Are you out of your mind?"

"You should realize why, but if you don't, I don't see why it's necessary to explain," he said.

Nevertheless, he now found himself wondering what had ever impelled him to go to the police. After all, it had been a mad thing to do. It even began to occur to him that the reasons he had given himself at the time were not the real reasons. This thought, however, did not disturb him. It actually heightened his sense of recklessness. He was more pleased than ever over his unconscionable behavior. There

Chapter 13

seemed to be enormous possibilities in sheer impulse. Perhaps he had really hit upon a new way of life!

Sylvia observed the mop handle lying across a soapy puddle that had accumulated around the pail. She held her hand out to Sydney without looking at him.

"Give me a cigarette."

He passed her his pack.

"Match?" she said.

He searched his pockets and produced a book of matches which he held out to her.

"You might at least light it for me," she said.

"It's hard for me to think of you that way," he said. "You always struck me as a very capable girl. The type with ten fingers on each hand."

"Don't be funny."

He lit the cigarette for her. "Every man has a streak of meanness in him," he said. "Even me."

"What'll I do?" she asked. "What can I tell him?"

Sydney frowned. "Who said you had to tell him anything?" A new thought occurred to him. "Besides, it's none of your business anyway."

This unexpected declaration brought a look of amazement to her features. "None of my business? But—"

"Just that," he said. "Because what I do is *my* business. He doesn't have to know about it—unless I want him to. Are you under an obligation to tell him everything you know? Stick to your typing. Make sure his manuscripts are nice and neat. That's where your responsibility ends. And anyway he probably won't be around much longer for you to do his typing, so you can consider that ended too."

"Just listen to him order me around," Sylvia exclaimed. "Allow me to remind you that what I do is my business too. And if I want to tell him, I'll tell him without any approval from you."

Sydney laughed disconcertingly. He realized so keenly that whatever he had to lose now was not worth having anyway, that he was prepared to venture even further. "Sure," he said. "Who said no? Go ahead and tell him. Only don't ask me what to tell him. It's your business."

She pulled a chair free of the furnishings on the bed and set it down on the floor facing him. Seating herself, she too began to laugh. "I just realized," she explained. "I don't really want to tell him either. After all, why should I?"

"Poor Fred," Sydney intoned with mock sadness. "This is a black day in his life. You can tell him that, all right. At least, somebody ought to tell him something."

"Oh, shut up," she said. "You needn't crow so much. You sound like a jackass."

"That makes me a very peculiar crow," he said, shaking his head. "What a metaphor."

For a moment she silently watched the smoke from her cigarette ascend. Her face was heavy with concentration.

"Sydney—listen."

"Sure," he said.

She presented her face to him, holding it at a peculiar oblique angle that resulted in an odd mixture of coyness and gravity. "I just had an idea."

"What?"

She placed her hands on his knees, leaning closer to him in a sudden avowal of intimacy. "Sydney, why don't you marry me?"

Her words appeared to magnetize him, holding his head on a line with hers so that their eyes continued to meet, although he was actually listening and not seeing her at all, the constantly repeated echo of her question requiring so much of his attention that there was only a modicum of consciousness left over with which he might feel the warmth of her hands lying flat and heavy on his knees.

Then came a reaction of fear as he felt his reckless mood escaping him. For the mood, having secured for him this, his ultimate triumph, was at the same time canceled out by the triumph. He had counted too much on not caring. Because if he accepted the triumph and agreed to marry her, he would have something to care about. And then he couldn't afford to be reckless. So the recklessness would work for him only at the cost of surrendering what he really wanted.

He couldn't decide, therefore, what to say to her. He didn't know at all whether he would rather protect himself or risk taking what meant so much to him. The best he could do was to pretend that she was joking. With exaggerated solemnity, he pressed a palm to his chest. "This is so sudden," he said.

"The comedy's not necessary, Sydney. I'm serious. Why not? Why shouldn't you marry me?"

He crossed one leg over the other in a covert attempt to free himself from the silent insistent pressure of her hands on his knees. He had a strong urge to continue as he had, to brush her lightly aside, but somehow, he couldn't do it.

"Listen—what is this?" he asked irritably. "What brought all this on so suddenly?"

"Don't you want to marry me?"

There was no escape from that direct query. She presented herself in a way that could allow for no further misunderstanding.

"You know I want to marry you." In his surrender, he now felt an unanticipated joy. "Only—"

"Then Sydney—let's!"

"Only—it's hard to believe." Now that he had exposed himself, he couldn't resist the urge to make it complete. He yearned to perform some act of humility. Sliding from the bed, he lurched against the foot of her chair and dropped his head into her lap, clasping her hands tightly and closing his eyes.

She stared down at the head that lay so heavily in her lap and, motivated by a sudden impulse of pity. she slipped one of her hands free from his and tenderly stroked his hair.

Chapter 14

Archie, hearing the key grate in the lock, dropped the book he had been reading, rolled off the bed and started for the door. He checked himself as Fred entered before he could reach for the knob.

"Oh, it's you. You got back fast."

Fred closed the door by leaning heavily against it. He brushed past Archie, not even looking at him, seeming by his preoccupation to dramatize the misery his bowed head and dragging gait unabashedly avowed. Stopping with his back to the armchair, he eyed the room for an instant as if to confirm his own location in it. Then he gripped the arms and with slow, agonizing care lowered himself into the seat.

Archie followed his roommate's maneuvers with apprehension. He waited until Fred, by dint of shifting and twisting, arrived at a permanent sprawled position in the chair. Then he returned to the bed, gingerly balancing himself on the edge of the mattress and leaning back on his hand.

"What's the matter?" he asked. "Didn't Brankowski like the chapter?"

Fred replied in a monotone of weariness. "It was all right. Any calls?"

"No." Archie wanted to ask if anything was wrong but some unfathomable shyness prevented him. "How about some coffee?" he suggested.

Fred waved a hand in refusal. "I thought maybe we'd hear something from the police by now," he said.

"Not a word," Archie assured him. "Tired?"

Fred shook his head. "I just heard a beaut from Brankowski's lawyer. I haven't gotten over it yet."

Archie rose from the bed and pulled one of the chairs away from the table. "What is it?"

"I put it to him as a hypothetical case," Fred went on.

"Yeah?" Archie said, straddling the chair and resting his folded arms on the back.

"Do you know what we can really get for owning that gun?"

Archie had a premonition of absolute disaster. His throat felt dry as he spoke. "The chair?"

Fred nodded. "You guessed it."

For a while there was silence. They were cut off from each other by the staggering realization which could not be grasped all at once, which could only be absorbed bit by bit. Archie, his chin poised on the back of his chair, glowered at the floor, his mind sodden with fear. When he raised his eyes, it was to see Fred stretched limply in the armchair, his body overburdened by its own weight as though each isolated conformation of flesh, each limb and muscle had abandoned its function in the body as a whole.

"You mean," Archie said, "if a murder is committed with a gun we own illegally, we're equally guilty, even if we know nothing about it?"

Fred nodded. "We're responsible for any death that's connected with the commission of a felony—like illegally possessing that gun. What I want to know is, did we make any remark to Giordano suggesting that he kill Phil White—even in joking, like 'take the gun' or 'kill Phil White'? I can't seem to remember."

"I don't know," Archie said. "I don't think so. But maybe we did. Why?"

Chapter 14

"The way I see it, it doesn't matter," Fred continued. "If Giordano feels like it, he can say we did anyway. What's to stop him?"

"What do you mean? What are you talking about?"

"That's what makes us liable for the death penalty along with the actual killer."

Archie's chair scraped the floor as he suddenly stood up. "It can't be. The guy doesn't know what he's talking about. What is he? A corporation lawyer? What the hell can he know about criminal law?"

Fred scornfully raised his eyebrows. "At least as much as you know. What difference does it make what kind of a lawyer he is? What he gave me was a definite law, not an interpretation of a law."

"Are you sure of that?"

"No, I'm an idiot like you. I have difficulty understanding English."

"What's the matter with you? Can't I even ask? What've you got against me now? Is it too much trouble to be pleasant?"

"Forgive me. I keep forgetting about your tender sensibilities."

Archie lifted his arms despairingly. "What's the use? You're so crazy in the head I can't even talk to you. Be reasonable a minute. It doesn't make sense. Maybe there is such a law, but did it ever occur to you that it only applies in extreme cases? We're not criminals. They won't give us the maximum. Can't you see that? Besides, how can they prove we told Giordano to take that gun, even in joking? Are they going to believe that lunatic?"

Fred drew his feet in close to the chair, shifting to face Archie whom he regarded with unmitigated disgust. "Go ahead—convince me. I'm the one that's going to sentence you. My neck isn't involved at all. What the hell are you ranting at me for? Don't you think I realize all that?"

"How should I know? You come in here, plop yourself down and calmly inform me that we're going to get the chair. The way you've been carrying on, I'm tempted to hire a psychiatrist as an interpreter. You're out of your head!"

"Maybe I am. And who wouldn't be with something like you around?"

Archie went to the closet. "I'll try to make life more bearable for you by getting out for a while." He removed his jacket from a hanger.

Fred pulled himself from the chair. "Hold on," he said. "You're not going out."

"I'm not?" Archie said. "And who says so?"

"Look—" Fred went up to him, holding out his hands. "I've got to go out again. We can't both go out. That cop said one of us has to be here all the time."

Archie defiantly slipped his jacket on and fastened the middle button. "So what? You were out this morning. I've got a right to go too."

"Listen," Fred pleaded. He had altered his tone to appeal to the other's altruism. "Just this once. This morning was business. I won't be gone long. I haven't seen Sylvia . . ." He dropped a hand on Archie's shoulder.

"The hell with you," Archie said, thrusting the hand away. "I should let you go screw around with Sylvia at a time like this? No thanks. I've been shut up here all day and I'm going out. When I come back you can go." He emphasized his determination by giving a final tug to his jacket and turning toward the door.

"Wait," said Fred. He sprang forward, caught at Archie's arm and pulled him from the door. "You're not going. You're not going to pull that childish stuff about whose turn it is when I—"

Archie whirled abruptly around and in twisting himself free inadvertently hurled Fred back against the side of the armchair. "Stay away from me, you crazy bastard."

Chapter 14

As Fred recoiled from the chair, his movement toward Archie, without being interrupted, became a rush. Red with anger, he struck his roommate a glancing blow on the side of the mouth. Archie shrieked unintelligibly. There was an instant's pause. Then he dropped his head and lunged, pounding his fists into Fred's stomach, forcing him back across the room until they both tumbled, panting, over the edge of the bed. Punching and grappling, they rolled across the mattress. All at once, Archie, who was on top, released his hold on Fred's arms and sprang back to the floor. There was a fleck of blood on his lower lip.

"Hold it! Hold it! It's all crazy. Cut it out!" he exclaimed.

Fred sat up slowly and rubbed a hand gingerly over his cheek. He looked coldly at Archie but made no move to continue the struggle.

"Go ahead," he said quietly. "Get the hell out."

"No," Archie said. "Go ahead. You go, if it means that much to you. What the devil do I care?"

Fred got off the bed. "Your lip's bleeding," he said.

"I know. It's nothing."

"Better wash it, anyway."

"Don't worry." He touched the cut and then looked at the red smear on his fingers. "You going out?"

Fred hesitated and looked thoughtfully toward the door. "Well—"

"Go on," Archie said, raising his voice in exasperation. "Don't get delicate with me now. When'll you be back?"

The heavy, bright afternoon sunlight fell about Fred like a veil, its glare shutting the street from view and almost suffocating him with its density. With short, choppy steps, he seemed to be fighting his way through it, keeping his head lowered and his shoulders drawn inward, his eyes stolidly fixed on the pavement directly before him. Some children were playing just beyond the doorway of the house and he almost stepped on a child's toy—a red fire engine—looming suddenly in his path. But he avoided it, almost shrinking from it as if it, too, were the harbinger of some nameless threat. He felt attacked by the very sounds of the street, exposed to something that came at him unseen through the glare.

A sense of having somehow diminished in size oppressed him. His body shook with fatigue.

His desire to see Sylvia had come upon him suddenly, almost without reason, at the moment he had returned home. The information provided by Brankowski's lawyer had given him a jealous feeling about himself. He found himself resentful of all encroachments. He wanted to disconnect himself from Archie, so his thoughts had turned automatically to Sylvia, regarding her as something specifically his own, something upon which he had set his inimitable personal stamp.

He hadn't seen her for a few days. He hadn't even thought of her. The detective's visit had driven him, along with Archie, into retreat. They had plunged into the Brankowski book, filling in the period of awful waiting almost in the hope that out of the activity itself would come an answer, an indication of some step to be taken that would extricate them from their impossible predicament. But the lawyer's opinion had radically altered things. Fred could no longer view the danger as a mutual one. With his own life at stake, the problem had suddenly become his own.

As he neared Sylvia's, he began to wonder why she had not even called him during the past days. It was unusual for her to ignore him for so long. He recalled that he had promised to see her an afternoon or so ago. He had completely forgotten. So she was probably angry. She had made another of her resolutions to break with him. But he

Chapter 14

knew her too well to be disturbed over her sulks. This would pass like all the others. His hold on her was solid.

Transformed by his present mood, he felt a kind of tenderness for her. They'd been together a long time. There was a lot of genuine affection between them.

He found himself across the street from her doorway. Perspiration ran down his face, making his unshaven cheeks itch. He crossed the street, touching with his fingers the aching spot below the eye where Archie had struck him.

As he rang Sylvia's bell, he recalled once more that she would be in a sulk. It was too bad. He was just beginning to realize what he had come for. He hoped he wouldn't have to fight for that too.

Chapter 15

Fred could tell at once from the way she greeted him that something was wrong. She had never pronounced his name just like that, as though it were an expletive forced from her lips as a consequence of being startled. He remained standing in the hallway, staring at her through the open door as if to let her know that he suspected something.

"Well," she said. "Aren't you coming in?"

He entered and stopped close to her, wary, but wondering at the same time if he liked her hair the way she had it pinned up. He could see smudges on her face. The torn dirndl and the sandals on her soiled feet completed an attractive picture for him.

"What are you looking at?" she said, closing the door.

"I've just decided that seediness is becoming to you. It wouldn't be a bad idea if you stopped using make-up. You do pretty well *au naturel*."

"I can understand why *you'd* like it," she said. "I'm in the middle of housecleaning. What do you want?"

"My, what a cold reception. Are you through with me forever—again?"

Without waiting for her reply, he went on past her through the foyer to the room ahead. He stopped at the threshold, dismayed to find everything so disarranged. The furniture piled on the bed and the still damp floor gave him a feeling of physical discomfort.

"Housecleaning?" he repeated. "It looks more like reconstruction to me."

She sidled past him into the room. "Maybe it is."

He caught her sly inflection. "All right. I give up. What're you supposed to mean by that?"

She looked at him curiously. "Fred—your face! What happened to you?"

He touched the red spot on his cheekbone. "Oh, that." He shrugged. "Nothing much."

"Did the police do it?" she demanded.

Her inordinate agitation puzzled him. "The police?" He peered at her uncertainly. "What makes you think—?" He advanced a step and stopped. She had retreated several paces. Her behavior astonished him.

"Why should the police do anything to me?" he demanded accusingly.

"I don't know. I—"

"Has anyone been here? From the police, I mean."

"No."

"Are you sure?"

"Of course I'm sure. What are you looking so—so frightened about?"

He let some of the tightness go out of his shoulders and chest. "Me frightened? What about you? If you haven't been up to something—" He advanced unexpectedly, caught her by the wrist and pulled her close. "What made you ask me about the police?"

His fingers tightened painfully about her wrist. She was forced to stand there and face him. But now, for the first time, she was in a position to see him in a way she never had before. In being committed to Sydney, she was left free enough to observe in Fred—or at least convince herself that she observed it— the fear that lurked behind his familiar truculent manner. The very thing that had always fascinated her in Fred, that soft expression in his eyes, now became the means of resisting him. She had previously taken that expression as a sign of sensitivity and warmth. She had once told him that he had eyes like a doe. Their rich pigmentation seemed always on the point of dissolving. However, it was not warmth, she now suspected, but anticipation of hurt. They were frightened eyes, the eyes of a creature perpetually hunted so that they had acquired a habit of looking backward. She had once interpreted this tendency as a turning inward, the mark of an introverted personality. What she had regarded as gentleness, she now chose to identify as terror.

Only a short while had elapsed since Sydney had left. But she was now so completely committed to her new relationship that anything outside it could be viewed with great detachment. She was therefore able to resist Fred in a way that had never been possible to her before, although his unexpected arrival had at first automatically produced her fear reaction.

His painful hold on her wrist helped to dispel her fear. She became uncompromisingly angry. Instead of making an effort to free herself, she gazed coldly at him, scarcely raising her voice as she challenged him: "Let go of me."

Her calmness made him feel foolish. He released her, turning awkwardly away as if to disavow his recent act. He followed this up almost immediately by an attempt to reestablish his old dominion, advancing on her once more with an air of refusing to be denied.

"Answer me," he said. "And give it to me straight. None of your lies. Why'd you ask me about the police?"

"What makes you so jumpy?" she asked. "Why are you so worried about the police?"

"Somebody's been here," he said, seizing her wrist again. "Talk—or I'll wring it out of you." His voice had become threatening.

"Please," she said, without altering her tone. "Don't get so dramatic. I'm busy cleaning and I want to get through." She pointed to the space on the bed Sydney had occupied earlier. "Sit down there and cool off."

His hand fell to his side. "Listen—" he began weakly.

She turned away from him to pick up the water bucket which was standing under the window. "I want to get through," she repeated. "I'm expecting someone in a little while."

She pulled aside the curtain separating the room from the kitchenette and dumped the contents of the bucket into the sink. He stood there glaring, wanting to act, yet not at all certain how to proceed. She knew something. He was sure of that. Getting it out of her had become a challenge. For he could see now how much was at stake—in the way she moved, with the cold hostility of inattention.

In considering his next move, he gradually became less aware of her. Consequently, he was unprepared for the way she turned from the sink, her face suffused with a darkening rush of blood, her movement sharp, sudden, reflexive, like a panic-stricken animal who in the instant of reacting has not yet decided upon flight or attack. It was almost as if she didn't trust herself to maintain the struggle too long. It had to be ended now or she would finally have to succumb as she had so many times before.

"Why don't you leave me alone?" she shouted. "Why did you come here? I won't answer a lot of questions about things I never had anything to do with. Get out of here! Get out or I'll call the police and tell them everything!"

And then she stopped, startled by her own outburst, drawing back from him and almost tripping over the bucket she had left standing just outside the kitchenette curtain.

He was more deeply shocked by her threat than her outburst. How much did she know? How much did she merely imagine?

Chapter 15

"You're crazy," he said, holding out his hands with the intention of calming her. Still shaken by his recent quarrel with Archie, he felt a strong urge to give up and get out of the place. But he responded to the demands of intelligence, knowing, in spite of his desire to get away, that he had to soothe her and learn what it was she claimed to know.

"Tell the police what?" he said. "What kind of insane ideas are you getting about me? Say—do you think I killed Phil White?"

She stood in a corner of the room, too intent on not giving in to listen to him. "Get out of here," she repeated.

He laughed to show his contempt. "I'll get out when I'm ready. Really, the indignant lady isn't very becoming to you. You should express yourself more sluttishly. It's closer to your real character. Something like 'scram'! That would be better suited to the natural vulgarity of your temperament."

As he spoke, he watched her break away from the corner, snatch her purse off the bureau, and run toward the door. For a moment, he tried to brazen it out. He made no move to stop her.

"Go ahead," he said. "Phone the police. Better tell them to hurry or I might knock your teeth out."

She opened the door and entered the outer hall. He waited, wondering whether she would really telephone. Perhaps the whole thing was a bluff. He could think of nothing she really had on him. Then he heard the clink of the coin in the metal box.

He ran quickly into the hall. She was standing at the phone with the receiver off, and waiting. He thrust her violently away from the instrument. The receiver, dangling from its wire, struck the wall. He caught it up and replaced it. Then, before she could escape him by way of the stairs, he seized her by the arm and began to drag her back to the apartment.

"Let go of me," she exclaimed.

"Please," he said, continuing to pull her toward the door. "I've got to talk to you. It's very important. Sylvia—think of what you're doing."

"Let go."

He stopped pulling but held onto her arm. "I'll let you go," he promised. "But, come inside. Just listen to me a moment. Then if you have to phone, I won't stop you. I'm not asking much, you goddamned little bitch!"

When he had released her, she stood rubbing her arm where his fingers had left faint bruises on the skin. Her face was immobile, her eyes like stones. He could tell nothing of what she was thinking.

"Will you come inside?" he said, scarcely moving his lips. She pushed past him and reentered the apartment. He followed quickly to prevent her from locking him out.

"Well—" she said, facing him, her hands on her hips.

He made a gesture of supplication. "Why won't you tell me?"

"What can I tell you that you don't know?"

"What were you going to tell the police?"

"You know very well—" She hesitated and appeared to be studying him. "I'll tell you," she said finally. "If you tell me something."

"Sure," he said. "Anything. I haven't got any secrets."

"What happened to your gun?"

"What gun?" he demanded. "Has Giordano—" And at the same instant, he remembered what had slipped his mind completely until this moment. It had been almost a year ago that he had shown the gun to her. How could he possibly have forgotten that she'd seen it?

"You know very well what gun. That twenty-two pistol you bought last year."

"Why—you're crazy. Do you think it was *that* gun? Anyway, it's gone. I lost it or something. Months ago. Besides, it was only good for blanks. You couldn't kill anyone with that thing."

Chapter 15

"Don't lie to me."

"But it's true. That was a blank-cartridge gun."

"Are you a filthy liar! Now I'm sure you're covering up. Why you showed me the bullets yourself."

"Sure I did. They were blanks."

"You told me they were real."

He shrugged. "I was kidding."

"They weren't blanks," she said. "I may not know much about guns but I know real bullets when I see them."

"You're crazy."

"All right. I'm crazy." She turned wearily away.

"Well—" he said, "how about telling me what you were going to tell the police?"

"What happened to your gun?" she answered.

"Why the hell can't you believe me? I'm telling the absolute truth."

"Do you think I can't tell when you're lying after all this time? What do you take me for?"

"Did you tell anybody about that gun?" he asked.

"You mean—the one with the blank cartridges?"

"Answer me. Did you mention it to the police?"

"No. I didn't."

"What were you going to phone the police about?"

"Will you please go?"

"Will I please go," he mimicked. "What is this all of a sudden. Say that to me once more and I'll knock you flat on your ear."

"You dare make one move toward me," she said, "and I'll get someone to beat you to within an inch of your life."

He laughed. "Who? Sydney?"

"Yes," she said, "Sydney!"

"Well, your uncle Charley certainly grew to heroic proportions all of a sudden. Has he been taking lessons?"

"Oh, are you in for a nasty surprise."

"Now where have I heard that before?"

"This time—you'll find out."

"Why don't you marry him and get it over with? You have so much imbecility in common, you'd make a lovely pair."

"I am going to marry him," she said.

"Allow me to congratulate you. I've a wonderful idea for a wedding present for him. He'd love it. A pair of horns."

"Better try them on yourself," she said.

"What?"

"You heard me. After all, you earned them."

"What do you mean?"

"And what's more—we are going to be married. We're getting our blood tests tomorrow."

His hands which had been resting in his pockets came to life and started to stroke the top of his head, each moving alternately across the broad, denuded scalp. Simultaneously, his lower lip protruded giving him a sulky expression like a disturbed child's alternative to tears.

"You really are?" His voice had dropped to the lower register, giving to his inflection the tone of announcing rather than questioning the fact.

"You seem surprised," she said. "I thought you would be."

He sat down on the edge of the bed, looking up at her with a flash of his former aggressiveness, "So you've already sampled his technique in bed."

"I decided to take your advice," she said.

He held his head in his hands and stared silently at the floor while making an effort not to feel what it was already too late to stop.

"Don't look so tragic about it," she added, resisting an impulse to pity him.

"All right," he said. "This is your big moment. At least you can tell me what that other stuff is about—about the gun."

She considered for a moment. "Listen, Fred—you were lying about that gun, weren't you? Those were real bullets you showed me?"

Chapter 15

"Well, what of it?"

"Where is the gun?"

"I told you the truth about that. It disappeared."

"It wasn't you then? You didn't kill Phil White?"

"Are you crazy? What the hell's going on here?"

"Well, the police happen to know you own the gun. Wait a minute, I didn't tell them."

"Then who did?"

"I don't know."

"How do you happen to know all this?"

"There was a detective here the other day. He told me. He asked me if I'd ever seen it. Of course, I denied everything. That's the truth."

"It must've been Giordano," he said.

"Did Giordano know about it?"

"Know about it! That son of a bitch killed Phil White. I'd stake my life on it."

"How do you know?"

Fred shrugged. "Just a hunch."

"Did Giordano use your gun?"

He hesitated. "As far as I know, Giordano stole it. But that's why I can't tell the police. I can get the chair just for owning that gun. You understand?"

"The chair," she repeated, incredulous. "My God!"

"If you say a word to anyone," he said.

"Of course not. Not even Sydney."

"Sydney," he repeated. "What a laugh."

She stiffened. "Don't eat your heart out."

"For you? Don't worry. Sydney's welcome to what's left."

"You'd better go now," she said.

He got up. "Sure. Give my love to Sydney."

Without answering, she watched him walk slowly toward the door. He stopped and looked back from the threshold.

"Would you—"

"What?"

"How about a farewell kiss?" he said. "Then I can go home and weep."

"Don't be a damned fool," she said.

He gave her an exaggerated bow and went out.

Chapter 16

For some moments after Fred's departure, Archie sat in the armchair, his immobility suggesting an identity with that object so that what was himself and what was chair seemed indissolubly merged. His face had acquired an evenness of color, varying only in its highlights, like something out of a monochromatic film. The rigidity with which he held himself was further repeated in the tightness of his features which appeared to be so stretched across his skull as to give them a sharpness foreign to their normal character. The fleshy tip of his nose which ordinarily dipped toward contact with his thin and extruding upper lip was now absorbed upward into the more cartilaginous structure of the nose as though the requirements of tension had exhausted all the slack.

This shell into which he had converted his flesh served not as an armor against penetration from the outside but as a barrier against the irruption of his own insides. Containing himself in this manner, he sought to cope with the information Brankowski's lawyer had given Fred.

He had first reacted to the notion of his own death in the electric chair as absurd. By degrees, absurdity had diminished to improbability. Finally, he had been able to accept this threatened death as possible. He had now to acquire some means of facing this possibility.

In a movement from which the rest of his body appeared detached, he raised his arm, bringing his hand to his head so that the tips of his fingers touched just above his temples at the beginning of the hair line. The hand now began a slow stroking motion across the scalp, its rhythmic and mechanical character suggesting a kind of external accompaniment to his thoughts, as if it were necessary to set a tempo sufficiently slow for their clear perception.

What could he think of this spontaneous obtrusion of life's end at what to him appeared to be still its mere beginning? It struck him sadly that there was no regular path for getting out of life as there was for getting into it. Birth, he realized, was always the beginning, but death could come long before the end. Was there some way of allowing this truth to exist without its being so painful?

His body, contracted within the chair, had suddenly become too small for his feelings to occupy. His thoughts seemed to be crowding into the space required by his lungs. His breathing became more rapid. He rose from the chair and moved aimlessly about the room, finding some relief in committing himself to this larger space.

Seeking rest from his thoughts, he permitted his eyes to concentrate on the objects about him. He dwelt on the detail of a lamp's broken plug, tracing back along the twisted, dust-laden wire to where it emerged at the base. His gaze climbed the fluted wooden shaft to where the shade hung at an awkward angle and a section of the wire frame jutted from the cracked parchment.

His attention wandered promiscuously to the bed whose coverings lay in a gnarled heap, their disorder telling of the recent struggle that had shaped them. His eyes continued to roam, giving to the disparate objects not merely their own character but that of their relations to each other so that the room itself gradually assumed a shape and aspect of its own, altogether distinct from any previous conception of it. It took on a quality separated from his associations with it, until it became a place that he viewed now for the first time. It was an experience Archie had known with various words, the repetition of which had directed attention first to the individual character of their components, their sound, their letters, until the word was stripped of reference or meaning, an object with a completely independent existence.

Turning again to the lamp, he no longer saw it as part of the room's familiar lineaments, but as broken shade, fluted shaft and straggling wire, a battered, paint-peeled and dusty object. So it was with the bed. It was nothing he had ever slept in.

He turned back to the armchair. An ash tray was balanced on one of the arms, its rim overflowing with the litter of half-smoked cigarettes. He picked a burnt match from the contents and twisted it speculatively between his fingers. Strange, he was thinking, how all these objects with their various parts make up this room. Remove one tiny thing, isolate the merest fragment and the room becomes different. He fixed his musing gaze on the match and scraped off the charred end with his thumbnail.

"There," he told himself, speaking aloud. "Now it's a different match."

It began to occur to him that every act made a difference. The step he took toward the chair, the movement from the door, each had its profound effect on every subsequent act. Life was shaped instantly and continuously. Perhaps then the answer to death not being the end was in this—this match stick. One could not choose one's death, but one might, if every act were taken seriously, be able to influence one's dying. Death could not be deferred, but it could be shaped. Thus, it could become bearable.

He broke the match stick in two with his finger. Aloud he said: "Perhaps, then, my holding onto this match stick and breaking it—this is life. And if I really know that this is what I'm doing, I can manage somehow to hang onto life."

He sat down again. His face had relaxed under the modulating influence of this new idea. Then it had not been dying that he had feared, but not living. It was not knowing, not feeling that had terrified him and he had merely projected that into the idea of death. But really—was it so simple?

His mouth stretched into a yawn. His head fell against the back of the chair. The weight of his body, the oneness of it, gave him a foolish feeling of joy.

He had fallen asleep. And it seemed as though he had closed his eyes hours ago. Actually, it had been only a few minutes, Fred was bending over the chair, nudging him.

"What is it?" Archie said, startled.

"You awake?"

Archie brushed a hand across his face. "Wait a minute," he said. He closed his eyes in an effort to recapture some fleeting memory. Then he lifted his head and looked about eagerly as though the room itself were the confirmation of what he sought. He cleared his throat and raised his eyes past the wall of Fred's body which pressed against the chair arm. He gazed briefly into Fred's face and then in confusion withdrew his glance to the body again.

Archie now shook off the last remnants of sleep, sat stiffly upright and said in a tone meant to disavow intrusion: "What's the matter?"

Fred's eyes were like the extension of some inner shadow. The lids, half closed, were patterned with tiny wrinkles. His expression appeared more an act of concealment than an admission of pain. But to Archie, who knew him so well, it clearly signified all it was meant to hide.

"You can go out now, if you like," Fred declared, his words sounding like a lame substitute for a different statement suddenly reconsidered.

Chapter 16

"When did you get back?"

"Just now." Fred turned so that a fragment of profile was all he presented to Archie of his face.

"How's Sylvia?"

"Dizzy as ever." This was announced with such a marked transposition from gravity to indifference as to direct Archie's attention to its motive rather than its meaning.

"By the way," Fred added, presenting his full face again but keeping it in such continuous movement as to prevent any focus on its expression. "Did you put something on your lip?"

Archie probed the cut with his tongue. "There's a little lump but it doesn't bother me. How long were you out?"

"Not long." Fred removed his tie and dropped it on the bed.

Archie, in the midst of his aroused sympathy for whatever Fred was feeling, was able to view the casting off of the tie with some disengaged part of himself, finding in it an amusement that was rather unusual. It was so characteristic an act on Fred's part that Archie's present objective observation of it made him conscious of how removed he had already become from his customary surroundings. He was thoughtful for a moment, considering whether Fred, who would tell him nothing, actually wanted him to persist in asking.

"How come you got back so soon?" Archie finally said.

"I left by Sylvia's request."

"She threw you out?"

"Look at me," Fred exclaimed. "A rejected lover."

"Are you serious?"

Fred nodded. "She's getting married."

"No."

"To Sydney."

"Life goes on, doesn't it?"

"What do you mean?"

Archie shrugged. "Nothing—just a remark. Listen, I don't think you should let it bother you so much."

"Who said it's bothering me?"

"Anyway, you've been urging her to do just that for a long time."

"Did I ever dream she'd do it?"

"Well, you weren't in love with her."

Fred sat down and held his head in his hands. "I don't know."

Archie lit a cigarette and dropped the match on the floor. A stem of smoke rose crookedly from his mouth. After a moment, he observed:

"Fred, it's painful. I know that, but—" Here he made an impetuous little gesture, turning his hand over from the wrist, flipping it as though signifying a tossing aside of some trivial thought. "But it seems to me rather mixed up, as if you were feeling for Sylvia what you really should be feeling for yourself."

"What?"

"I mean it. I just realized that you never allow yourself to feel what you want to feel. You always have to disguise it as if it were connected with something else. It's funny how clear it is. When you left, I was sitting here thinking about dying. And I was thinking about death as though it were some catastrophe that was about to happen to me. Until, all of a sudden, I realized that it was *my own death*, exactly the way this is my own arm and leg and body. You see what I mean?"

Fred appeared to be considering some mocking retort. His face had taken on the expression that usually preceded such a response. But something in Archie's manner made him hesitate

"The fact is," Archie continued, "I've been deciding something in my own mind about all this. I don't think we ought to wait any more. We've been too cautious. And by that I mean we've been too ready to be afraid of what's hap-

Chapter 16

pened, I—" He stopped, realizing that his way of presenting what was on his mind wasn't making much sense.

"You're funny," Fred said, "when you get these streaks."

Archie smiled and a nostalgic expression appeared on his face. "Well, I guess I don't blame you." He rose and took his coat from the back of a chair.

"Going out?" Fred asked.

Archie nodded. "Maybe if I tell you where I'm going, you'll understand better what I was trying to say."

"For Christ's sake, don't be so mysterious."

"I'm going to Giordano's."

"What?"

"It's about time," Archie said.

"You're impossible to figure out; you know that?"

Archie lingered at the door. "I wish I could make you understand."

"Why?" Fred waved him off. "I don't give a damn anyway."

"Because you still keep thinking it's Sylvia. That's where you're wrong. That's what I've been trying to make you see."

"Stop worrying about me. I can get along without the help of your intuition."

"All right," Archie said. He opened the door.

"What are you going to do?" Fred asked. "Put it to him pointblank about the gun?"

"I don't really know."

Fred shrugged. "You're crazy in the head."

Archie nodded as he went out. "Maybe I am. But that isn't so bad. I can think of worse things."

The night threatened rain. A shabby pink sky hung low over the rooftops. The atmosphere was so laden with moisture as to give it an additional quality of mass as though it had been heaped up in the streets to await disposal by the coming storm. Seen through the dense, inert weight of air, the buildings acquired by contrast an insubstantial aspect as if they had served some temporary requirement of the day, of whose recent departure they now appeared the mere leftovers.

Such a night was well suited to Archie's mood which was insular and aloof. He disdained connection with anything external at the same time that his separation gave him a clearer sense of what went on beyond that perimeter now so jealously his own. And everything around him tended to confirm his own sense of permanence. By the time he knocked at Giordano's door, any lingering doubts about the rightness of this visit had been dissipated.

He waited, and since there was no immediate response to his knock, he struck the door again, using his fist to pound several times in succession so that the sound echoed shatteringly through the hall.

The door opened and Giordano, holding a handful of brushes, peered out. "Why don't you smash the door down?" he grumbled.

Archie stepped from the shadows. "You busy?"

"Oh!" Giordano's anger was replaced by recognition. He waved the brushes in a welcoming gesture. "Sure I'm busy. If you were the King of Siam, I wouldn't let you in. But I'll make an exception of you. Come on in."

Archie followed him into the studio where a fluorescent lamp suspended by wires from the ceiling gave to the room a ghastly, sterile color, consistently coating everything. Giordano's own heightened pallor made him seem like an ambulant addition to the ghostly furnishings. Archie peered painfully about. He felt as if a glaze had been laid over his eyes. Blinking, he made out the cot at the far end and started toward it.

Chapter 16

Giordano slammed and bolted the studio door. "That's to keep out visitors," he explained. "One in particular. I'm being persecuted by a lousy detective. And I haven't made up my mind whether to let him in if he comes back."

"A young guy?" Archie asked. "Dark, and kind of nervous?"

"That could be the guy."

Archie sat down. "It must be the same one who came to see us. Said his name was Brown. He was looking for that pistol. I told him to try here." He looked challengingly at Giordano as he spoke.

"That's what I thought," the painter said. "I don't know whether I should get sore about that or not. I keep thinking you should have come here first and asked me."

"Tell me," said Archie. "I'm still not sure. Did you borrow that pistol from us or did you steal it?"

"Go ahead. Be whimsical. But the right thing would've been for you to come over long ago. I won't make an issue of it now. As long as you finally did come, I can clarify you."

"That's what I came for."

"I guess you figured right away that Phil was killed with your gun."

"Wasn't he?" Archie demanded.

"Now take it easy," Giordano said evasively. "What do you expect me to do, sit down and sign a confession? The trouble is, you don't take an intellectual attitude toward the problem."

"Get the idea out of your head that I came here to fool around, Giordano."

"You don't understand me," Giordano said. "I'm not fooling around. Murder, one doesn't fool around with. But you think you can walk in here and drag it all out of me. That isn't how I do things. How did I act when you came in here? Wasn't I friendly? Why? Don't you think I knew why you came? All right. Try to get this through your head. Before I trust myself to you, I want to be understood. Is that asking too much?"

"Now I'll tell you something," Archie said. He rose from the cot and went toward Giordano who leaned against the back of the red leather chair. "When all this happened—the first few days—I was in a terrible panic. That was before I knew how seriously involved I was. I was actually afraid to come here. I even had an idea that you might take a shot at me."

Giordano chuckled. "Very complimentary. I feel like a character out of the Renaissance."

"It was today for the first time," Archie went on, "that I learned I could get the chair just for owning that gun. At first, I was really terrified. I can't tell you how much. Then I started to think about it. I really sweated it through. Maybe you'll believe me when I tell you I've just been through an experience I'll never forget."

"I've got to admit it," Giordano said. "This isn't quite what I expected. I wasn't sure how I'd handle you if you came over. It's funny, isn't it, the way these things turn out."

"Well, what about it?"

"All right," Giordano said nervously. He moved around the chair and stopped. His eyes restlessly circled the room. Finally, he went toward the window and stopped before an orange crate lying on the floor under the sill. After a moment, he rose, holding something in his closed hand. "Our everyday selves aren't equal to the occasion," he said. "This requires a state of greater disinterest."

Archie watched the painter with apprehension, expecting that the other was about to produce the missing gun. "What is it?" he asked.

Chapter 16

Giordano approached and held something out on his palm. "Here," he said. "I came into a piece of luck. The best stuff I've ever had."

He proffered two thin cylindrical rolls wrapped in pink rice paper. They were the length of an ordinary cigarette but appreciably smaller in diameter.

"Tea," Archie exclaimed.

"And not the garbage Phil White tried to put over on me either. I made a new connection. This is the stuff! Real African jive!"

Archie discerned something in Giordano's face that checked the sardonic comment he had been about to make. Instead, he smiled, not at the painter but at his own belated understanding.

"Why you're high already," he said.

"I had to get down into myself," Giordano said. "I've been high for three days." He turned toward the racks where he stored his canvases. "Here, I'll show you why," he added, pulling one of them out and placing it on the easel for Archie to see. He stood beside the painting and pointed dramatically:

"Look at that! Look what's going on there!"

Archie frowned. "I don't know," he said. "I've seen you do better."

"Are you mad?" Giordano exclaimed. "Why I've completely smashed the rigid boundaries of painting. It's like—" He stopped and thrust a reefer at Archie. "Here—light up, will you? How can you appreciate anything like this without being in the proper condition? It's like asking a cockroach what he thinks of the universe."

He pressed the reefer into Archie's hand and struck a light with a match he had taken from his pocket. He held the flame ready, standing before Archie, insistent and excited until the latter reluctantly bit off the sealed end of the reefer. Giordano applied the match. Archie inhaled deeply, his face reddening with the effort and his chest swelling like a sponge suddenly immersed in water. Straining to keep the smoke in his lungs, he passed the reefer back to Giordano who drew on it with a loud sucking sound.

After a bit, Archie gave an explosive exhalation. "Good tea," he gasped.

Giordano nodded, his cheeks bulging with the effort to hold the smoke.

"Better than Phil's catnip," Archie added, deliberately attempting to provoke the other.

Giordano exhaled and shook his head with disgust. "Don't remind me of the bastard. You should've seen me with that stuff. I lit one after the other till I got blue in the face. I couldn't believe he'd pull a low stunt like that on me. I was his buddy. I thought it was my fault. I thought I couldn't get high anymore."

Archie, who had taken another puff, made a spluttering sound with his lips as he expelled his breath in an involuntary spasm of mirth. "Hold it," he exclaimed. "You're killing me. I get a vision of you puffing yourself into a brilliant cerulean blue." He chuckled hysterically. "Do you know what you look like to me with a blue face?"

Giordano watched him curiously. "Don't tell me you're high already."

"I guess I am. It's powerful stuff."

"I told you. It's one-puff tea. Way out!"

"Green stuff?"

"No, this is brown. It's African. It might even be hash. You can blow your top on one puff. It's almost too powerful."

Archie seriously regarded the reefer which he held between his fingers. "I'll say it is."

"There's such a thing as having tea that's too powerful," Giordano explained. "I don't like tea that I can't work under." He turned to stare at his painting and became suddenly silent, his face gathering a look of troubled intensity.

Chapter 16

He behaved as if he saw not the canvas itself but some irreducible living shape imprisoned there. A puzzled frown exaggerated the lines in his pale, shrunken face. He seemed under that blighting fluorescent glare like a creature on the verge of retreat from something too intangible to be anything less than frightening.

Archie could feel the light beating down on him in waves. His mouth felt dry. "I think I'm blowing my top," he said softly.

"Look at that thing," Giordano said in a strained whisper. He pointed at the canvas and turned to Archie with his eyes bulging as though in an effort to conquer the overpowering brightness by absorption.

"Christ," Archie muttered. "It's mad. What kind of a painting is it?"

Giordano shook his head. He appeared struggling to lift himself above some level of obsession. "What is it? What is painting?" he demanded. "I'll tell you. It's my direct struggle with reality—with things, with space." He paused and seemed to make an effort to continue. "Without it, I wouldn't be able to purify, to know clearly the things that are left over." He stalked toward Archie, his face taut. "Don't you see it?"

Archie regarded him in numbed silence. Giordano turned again to the painting, his voice rising. "Look at it! Slime and sediment!" He brought his hands together in a gesture of squeezing something. "Wrung out of life to make living clean enough to endure. What a monstrosity! Look hard at it! Isn't it horrible? There's all the filth of existence right before your eyes! God!"

Archie could make out the canvas only as a blur. He started walking toward the easel. Giordano caught at his sleeve and stopped him.

"Listen," Giordano said.

"Well?" said Archie.

Giordano's voice dropped to normal. "It's all right," he said, turning away. "I went off the beam for a moment."

"I'll say you did." Archie returned to the cot and sat down. "But I think I'm beginning to catch on," he added, frowning at his own uncertainty.

"Then you know what I'm talking about?" Giordano said.

He made a series of sharp, controlled movements with his hands as if to project something he couldn't express.

"Wait," said Archie, holding up his hand as he heard sounds from the direction of the door. "I thought there was someone out there. I—" He stopped as someone knocked. "Who's that?" he whispered.

Giordano frowned and got up. "I'll go see."

"How about the tea?" Archie said. "It must stink in here."

"Stink?" Giordano said. "Whoever it is should be grateful for such a heavenly reek."

Chapter 17

It took Giordano a few seconds to free the bolt. Then he swung the door wide and stared out at the detective whom he continued to regard for some moments before he was able to recognize him.

"Oh, I forgot about you," he finally said. He turned to Archie, standing well back in the studio against the cot. "It's that detective," he announced.

"Mind if I come in?"

"Shall I let him in?" Giordano asked Archie.

Archie came forward and peered through the doorway. "Hello," he said. The detective nodded to him.

"Why don't you let him in?" Archie asked.

Giordano remained standing in the doorway. "I don't have to unless he has a search warrant."

"I don't have a warrant," the detective said. "I just came to look around."

"Don't be stupid, Joe. Let him in."

Giordano stepped aside with obvious reluctance. "Watch out," he said to Archie. "It's another one of those friendly affairs. You know what I mean? Cop shakes hands with suspected killer? Welcome to the era of brotherly love." He turned on the detective to demand: "What do you mean, look around?"

The detective waved Giordano off. "Take it easy. You'll find out."

"You and I might be here on the same business," Archie said to the detective.

"What business?"

"Anything you have to say to Archie," Giordano interposed, "has to be on a high level. He's here to discuss life and death."

"Still clowning, aren't you, Giordano?"

"I never clown. Ask Archie."

"What I was about to say—" Archie began.

"Something's burning," the detective said, lifting his head and sniffing.

Giordano turned from locking the door to announce defiantly: "Arrest us, then. You've caught us red-handed."

"Calm down," Archie urged the painter. "Nothing's burning," he added. "It's marijuana."

"That's right," Giordano said, putting his arm protectively across Archie's shoulder. "Archie's innocent. You can't touch him. He's here for philosophical reasons only."

The detective smiled. "Now I see," he said to Giordano. "Hash! You're high as a kite."

Archie freed himself from Giordano's affectionate embrace. "Here, you're all right. You don't have to lean on me."

"You must've been high the last time I saw you," the detective continued.

Giordano gazed haughtily at the detective. "You say that as if you were Balboa discovering the Pacific. But why? Pure dissimulation. Fundamentally, you see me with the vulgar eyes of a cop." He began to grow eloquent. "You see me as a drug fiend, a man shorn of his senses and consequently an enemy of society. Arrest me then. Put me away. Shield your timid world from the devastating visions of my Olympian scorn. But remember—you cannot kill us all. There will be others to take my place. You and your kind,"

Chapter 17

Giordano went on, waving his arms oratorically, "will be swept away on the rising torrent and cast into—" he paused, stared absentmindedly at Archie and finished lamely with "the dust bin of history."

The detective and Archie exchanged embarrassed glances. "What did you want to tell me?" the detective asked.

"It's kind of hard to explain," Archie said. "Are you here about that gun?"

The visitor looked at his watch. "Why?"

Giordano stepped between them and turned his back on the detective. "Relax, Archie. You must realize I have a real affection for you. You can still be saved. You know why? Because you haven't gone the whole way yet. Like our friend here—" He pointed over his shoulder. "Our friend here is a seven year suicide. I pity the poor bastard."

"Sure," Archie said. "Sure." He made an attempt to slip past Giordano.

"No, don't. I'm not crazy. Listen to me," Giordano insisted.

"Who said you're crazy?"

"Why do you think this pitiful detective came here? Why? Because he doesn't realize it's too late. He's—"

"Cut it," Archie said. "You're raving. Don't you know that?"

The detective tapped Archie on the shoulder. "Never mind," he said. "Let him talk."

Archie shrugged. "Well, I guess it doesn't make any difference."

Giordano caught at Archie's arm. "Sure it doesn't make any difference," he said haughtily. "But it's a trick just the same."

"Of course," Archie admitted. "Something's up. I know that." He glanced quickly from Giordano to the other man, then back again. "But what do you care?"

"That's right," the detective said. "You can't lose anything by telling the truth. Go ahead and talk."

"A lot you care about the truth," Giordano said. "I know why you came here to snoop around. Shall I tell you why? You didn't come here to arrest me. You came here with a load of garbage—to dump it all on my doorstep. You saw my painting at Archie's house and decided I'd found a way of getting rid of garbage and you wanted to find out how I did it. You asked for the truth! Well, listen—"

He raised a hand toward the ceiling and turned his face up to the light, his pale features becoming even sharper, his eyes glowing. "I did it by giving up a lot more than you ever had. I had to kill a man, you see. I was removing myself from your world. I'm outside of it now. And you can't touch me and you can't even get anything from me because there isn't anything in you to follow me with. So why not arrest me? What are you stalling for? That's the only thing left for you to do. Because if you don't accept the fact that you're a detective and detectives have to arrest murderers, you haven't any reason for being here."

He caught the detective by the arm and led him across the room toward the easel. "Here, I'll show you what I mean. Take a look at that canvas. What do you see there?"

"I don't know. You tell me. I guess it's a good painting."

"Stop the crap," Giordano exclaimed. "It's lousy. It's no good at all. You know why? Because it doesn't make any difference any more as painting. I'm beyond all that. Whether it's good or bad, that's accidental. The world is stuffed up with critics, reviewers, professional art lovers who go around pinning their little good and bad labels on everything. It's all crap. It's all beside the point. It doesn't have anything to do with art. There's something else in there that I'm after—and it's not anything you'll ever be interested in. You're interested in a *good* painting. That's why you've come to the wrong place. That's why you have to remain a detective."

He thrust past the man and turned toward the window. "What's the use. You'll never understand me in a million years!"

Chapter 17

Archie, who had remained near the door, listening, drew his hands from his pockets and gazed at his palms. They were moist and marked with tiny ridges where his fingernails had bitten into the skin. He now moved in from the door with an awkward, tentative motion as if testing his legs. The detective had his back toward him as he stood near the easel, closely watching Giordano who leaned with his hands against the window frame, looking out.

Archie was certain something was about to happen. The detective wasn't there for nothing. Hadn't he deliberately goaded Giordano into confessing the murder? And now, he was obviously waiting for something else. Yet Archie realized that he wasn't particularly concerned. There seemed to be something more important involved. It was as though he had been inoculated with some of Giordano's madness. The most vital thing appeared to be what was happening to the painter. Still, he wondered at his lack of self-concern. Was it clarity or narcosis? The air of the room seemed poisoned. Yet he knew he had to see this thing through.

Giordano turned from the window and noticed the detective standing behind him, his head bent at an angle as he curiously studied the painting.

"What are you standing there for?" the painter demanded. "Why don't you do what I tell you?"

"What kind of painting is that supposed to be? Is it something out of your own life?"

"Archie," Giordano said. "Tell this poor bastard to give up. Tell him it's no use."

A sudden pounding on the studio door made the three of them start. Each stared guiltily at the source of the sound as if the jarring intrusion had turned his preoccupations into an act of shame.

Giordano and Archie instinctively turned toward the detective.

"It's all right. Don't try anything," he said.

"The police," Archie whispered with peculiar excitement.

"Open up!" came a voice from outside. The pounding was renewed.

"Better open," the detective said. "Hurry up."

"You ought to know," Giordano said.

"This is it," Archie declared, looking with tense satisfaction toward the door.

"The hell with all of you," Giordano announced. He snapped back the bolt and pulled the door open.

Two men entered. One held a leveled revolver. The other, dangling a pair of handcuffs, said to the painter:

"Joseph Giordano?"

"Yes," Giordano said.

The handcuffs were clamped neatly over his wrists. The other man put away his gun, muttered something unintelligible, slapped his side and called to the detective: "Well, if it isn't Sherlock himself. What were you trying to do, pull a grandstand play? You were supposed to meet us downstairs."

"I thought I might get something before you came busting in here with your handcuffs. I did, too, if it makes you feel any better."

The second of the two men now interrupted. "Always said you were too ambitious. One of these days, Brown, you'll double-cross yourself."

The detective smiled. "Well, what's wrong with trying?"

"That's something you wouldn't understand," said the man who had manacled Giordano. He motioned to his companion. "Come on, let's get out of here. Especially seeing as Sherlock has got the case all sewed up."

"What about me?" Archie said, addressing the detective they had called Sherlock.

"You come along too."

Chapter 17

One of the men thrust Giordano ahead of him through the door. Archie followed. The second of the newcomers looked back and pointed toward the easel. "What's that supposed to be? A painting?"

"Ask the guy who painted it," the detective answered. "He says it's just garbage."

"Well, Sherlock, I agree with him. Let's go."

Chapter 18

"The blowtop, he'll be put away in a place for the criminally insane. There isn't anything else we can do about him now. All you have to do is sign the statement." Inspector Sheean pushed the clipped sheets across his desk and Archie picked them up, glanced over them for a moment and dropped them back on the desk.

"I can't decide right away," he said. "It's complicated."

"You've got this thing all wrong. You're not doing us a favor. We're doing you one."

"I don't know," Archie said. "You haven't found the gun. So you haven't got anything on us. The lawyer said—"

"The hell with the lawyer. You think we've given up? Suppose that gun turns up? You know where you'll be then? We can prove it's your gun. That's a lead-pipe cinch. We can even make a case out of it now. The reason we won't—well, it's not worth the expense. We're not after you. You're not a criminal. You did something stupid by keeping that gun around, but things have worked out in such a way that we can give you a break. You sign this statement that the gun was yours and you saw Giordano take it, so we can tighten our case against Giordano and you walk out with a suspended sentence whether the gun eventually turns up or not. Now sign it and don't be a jackass!"

Archie picked up the papers again, fidgeted over them, reading an occasional paragraph, and then, still undecided, placed them carefully back on the corner of the desk.

"How's Giordano now?" he asked.

The man shrugged with easy indifference, presenting to Archie that face of the pure professional who has lived through innumerable similar situations and has learned how, with an effort, to achieve patience.

"He had a bad night of it," he said. "Why?"

"Will they be able to do anything for him?"

"It's hard to tell. The doctor said, possibly, with shock treatments. Still, it's a matter of maybe years." He glanced at the statement lying on the corner of the desk, then up at Archie's face. "You must have been pretty fond of him," he suggested.

"It isn't fondness exactly."

"He was a pretty smart guy. I guess that had something to do with it."

"Something," Archie admitted.

"I'll tell you ," the inspector went on. "The doctor said Giordano was comparing himself to God last night. It was a very strange thing he said. Something about being better than God because God could only create what never existed before. He said that was easy. He said the hard thing was to create something that you knew existed."

Archie was surprised. Why was the inspector telling him all this? What was his purpose? Was it something that interested him for its own sake, or was he trying to get at something else? Archie crossed his legs uncomfortably. He connected his feeling of bewilderment with an event in his boyhood when he had sat in the office of the school principal and instead of being scolded for the misbehavior that had brought him there, had listened to the principal go off on some seeming irrelevance. The inspector's office had the same dank odor that had permeated the school corridors.

Chapter 18

"Did he really say that?" Archie heard himself asking. It was as if a message had been smuggled to him through the official's lips. The meaning of those words was so private and yet so clear. Giordano, like himself, had tried to take what already existed and create it, that is, to make it into more than it was. He had tried, in short, to create his life. That was what he had meant by getting, as he called it, beyond life. So he must have arrived at the idea of creating death. It was as literal as that. Except that Giordano had tried to accomplish this by putting his life outside of himself, as though it were a painting. Thus, in committing murder, he became, like the tragic heroes, a man condemned, a man outside of life. Gun and painting and life had been the same things for the painter. That had been Giordano's confusion. He, Archie, by the grace of God, need not make the same mistake.

Archie now began to feel strangely free. Every act, every decision had to be his own. He alone could create his own being. It was like that match stick. Everything that happened to it made it different. He wasn't going to be the inspector's match stick, but his own match stick. Beyond that, nothing mattered.

"It's funny his saying that," the inspector went on. "It puts me in mind of something. Because like the ravings of any lunatic, there's a lot of truth in it. It's a pretty easy thing to go off on a tangent of your own. Anyone can do that. But doing what should be done—the right thing—that's a whole lot harder. That's what your blowtop friend must have meant. It's a funny thing that a guy in his position should understand it so well. Maybe he tried to live up to it more than he was able to. Some people, you know, are born weak and no matter how much they may try, they can't overcome it. That's one of the great tragedies of life. You see what I mean? An artist can get like that. Or maybe, because he's like that, he becomes an artist."

"I don't know," Archie said. "What are you trying to tell me."

"You can learn a lesson from your friend," the other explained. "You can still do the right thing and make it count. For him, it's too late." He flipped the paper toward Archie again. "Here—sign it."

Archie got to his feet. His mouth was set stubbornly. "No—I won't sign it. I won't touch it. It's a filthy trick. All this stuff you've just been telling me! Christ—how clever. How ingenious. I never imagined police were like that. Subtle—subtle as hell. But, you don't understand. I can't be fooled any more. Because I know now what Giordano meant. I don't think you do. You couldn't if only because you know so well how to use it for your own purposes. So—"

The inspector had also gotten to his feet. He now leaned across the desk with an indifferent smile. "So you think I'm subtle, do you, boy? Remember this, then. There might be a first degree murder charge at the end of your road. You know what that means. That's not subtle. Maybe you'd like that better."

"The electric chair? Sure," Archie said, "that exists all right." He gestured scornfully toward the paper on the desk. "That paper doesn't. That's why I can't put my name on it. You've got Giordano's confession that he's a murderer. Do what you like with it. It's no concern of mine."

"All right. I've tried to help you. It doesn't matter now. Frankly, I hope that gun doesn't turn up. Because if it does, God help you."

He waved his hand in a brusque gesture of dismissal. Archie turned and went out. A policeman who had been waiting for him outside escorted him down a long hallway, past a series of doors, to turn in finally at a small bare room with a barred window, a wooden table and a couple of chairs. Fred, in a dark suit, freshly shaven and looking paler than usual, broke off his conversation with the lawyer, a stout,

Chapter 18

bushy-haired individual in tweeds who sat on the table across from him.

"What happened?" Fred demanded.

"Hello, Mr. Friedman," Archie said, nodding to the lawyer.

"Your friend here was worried. I had a time trying to reassure him. Did they want you to sign a statement?"

Archie nodded. "I refused."

"What kind of a statement?" Fred demanded. "Does it mention me?"

"I didn't read it."

The lawyer slid off the table. He waved Fred off. "Now, now. Don't get upset. There isn't anything happened that can't be put right." He pulled one of the chairs from around the side of the table.

"Sit down, Archer. I want to explain a few things to you."

"You mean, I should've signed the statement?"

"I'm not saying you should sign anything," Friedman declared blandly. "Let your conscience be your guide, as they say. Here, sit down. I'll explain to you how things stand, and then you can make up your own mind about signing that statement."

"It doesn't make any difference," Archie said. He sat down. "You can explain, but my mind's already made up."

Fred stepped forward, holding his hands stiffly at his sides, his fingers bent tensely inwards. "What in hell's the matter with you?" His dilated eyes were reddened at the corners. The light falling on his face from the barred window revealed the pouches beneath his lower lids. "You talk like a madman. What are you trying to do?"

"Here," said Friedman, putting a hand on Fred's shoulder. "Let me handle this. He's no fool. He'll listen to reason."

Fred threw up his arms and strode to the window. "Reason! You don't know him. When he gets like this, you haven't got a chance. Go ahead, talk to him. You'll see. He's—"

"Then give him a chance," Archie interrupted. "And shut up. Let the man talk. Go ahead, Mr. Friedman. It won't make any difference, but at least I'd like to know how it all comes out."

"This is the way I see it," Friedman began softly. "I just spoke to the assistant D.A. He's an old friend of mine. Whatever's going on, he wouldn't hide it from me. He's too smart to do anything like that. He's a great guy. Well, he admitted he doesn't have much of a case. No one saw Giordano kill this guy. All he's got is the testimony of this girl and this fellow—what are their names?"

"Sylvia and Sydney," Fred said, turning from the window.

"Well, the girl can swear that the gun was yours. They might be able to establish that all right. Especially with Giordano admitting he took the gun from your house. Of course, with Giordano off his nut, we can shake that testimony up a bit. It may and it may not stick. Again, everything depends on finding that gun. Without it, they haven't got a chance. So here's how it shapes up. The D.A.'s office wants a conviction for the record. They want to get Giordano declared criminally insane. So if you sign the statement that it's your gun and you saw Giordano steal it, they practically guarantee you a suspended sentence. They get their conviction and Giordano goes to an institution where he'll be better off anyway."

"I see," Archie said.

"Now wait," Friedman admonished. "I'm not through yet. As I said, the gun hasn't turned up. It may never turn up. In that case, the whole thing'll have to be dropped. If they do find the gun, they'll still have a hard time making a case of it. But the assistant D.A. assures me that if you force him to go to trial in order to close the case, he'll try to make it as hot for you as he possibly can. In other words, he'll try to force a first degree murder conviction from the jury by showing that you instigated the murder. So you see, it's a

Chapter 18

gamble all around. Under the circumstances, I'd suggest that instead of having anything like that hanging over you, you sign the statement. You'll be free and clear. Giordano'll get the kind of treatment he needs at an institution and everybody's happy."

Archie nodded. "I see. But just one thing."

"Sure," Friedman said. "Take your time. Ask any questions you like. That's what I'm here for."

"If I refuse to sign the statement, they still can't touch Fred, can they?"

"Well, they can if they want to. But I don't think they'll get very far if you insist, as you suggested, that it's your gun and not his. The girl will testify that he claimed ownership of it, but I can demolish that simply by having Fred admit he was lying. Besides, he needn't have known it was a real gun. For all he knew, it was a blank pistol. But, as I say, it all depends on how much you're willing to take on yourself."

Fred turned from the window to inquire: "But suppose I claimed the gun was mine. I could sign that statement, couldn't I?"

Friedman shrugged. "Sure, I guess that would be all right."

"All I'd get would be a suspended sentence—right?"

The lawyer nodded. "That's the deal."

"In that case," Fred asserted, "if he won't sign it, I will."

"What do you think of that, Archer?"

Archie looked up in the midst of searching his pockets and said absently: "I must've left my cigarettes in the cell."

The lawyer proffered a pack. Archie took a cigarette and leaned toward the flame of Friedman's lighter.

"Thanks," Archie said. He inhaled with deep satisfaction.

"Are you going to sign that statement?" Fred demanded.

"No," Archie said complacently. "And neither are you."

"That's what you think."

"Now wait a minute," Friedman said. "Cool off here."

"Is there any way he can stop me from signing the statement?" Fred asked.

"No, how can he stop you? But before we go into that, I'd like to say just one thing more." Friedman looked gravely at Archie. "Do you think someone in Giordano's condition who killed a man in cold blood should be allowed to mingle in society?"

"How do you know he killed a man?" Archie demanded.

"Oh, a logician," Friedman said, winking at Fred. "Well, then, who killed Phil White? Giordano admitted it, didn't he?"

"If the mere confession isn't admissible as evidence in court, why should it be here?"

"Now look—don't be so stubborn," Friedman said, his face reddening under the increasing strain on his affability. "I've been in this business a long time. I think I ought to know what I'm doing."

"I'm sure you do," Archie said. "But I'm not in business."

"Never mind," Fred exclaimed. "The crazy bastard doesn't know what he's saying anyway. He's suddenly discovered a great principle. Can't you see—he's discovered the secret of the universe. Look at him—the smug idiot. Why waste time trying to convince him? He can't stop me from signing that paper. Let's get it over with."

"You heard what he said," Friedman told Archie sternly. "Is that how you want it?"

"He can't sign that paper," Archie said.

"Try and stop me," Fred retorted.

Friedman struck his palm against the table. "I've had enough of this. Is that your final word? Are you going to sign that statement, or shall I have Birnley here do it?"

Chapter 18

Archie stepped back toward the door and faced them, his eyes glittering above the bitter curve of his mouth. "If I go to the D.A.'s office this minute," Archie said, "and tell them I can put my hands on that gun, I don't think there'll be any statement to sign. So better think twice about it."

Friedman's mouth opened. His jawbones tightened under the soft flesh of his cheeks. "You crackpot," he exclaimed, his voice breaking as it leaped an octave beyond the range of his vocal poise. "Don't you get funny with me or I'll put you where you belong so fast it'll make your head spin."

"Don't believe him, Friedman," Fred intervened, pulling the lawyer back. "He's lying. It's a complete bluff. He doesn't know where that gun is anymore than I do."

"He doesn't?" Friedman demanded. "Then what does he mean by making such a remark? What does he think I am?"

"If you think I'm lying," Archie said, "just try to sign that statement."

"Don't fall for it, Friedman. He's just shooting off his mouth. Besides, what difference would it make if he did find the gun? If I sign the statement, then everything's settled whether the gun turns up or not."

Friedman shook a menacing finger in Archie's face. "Do you or don't you know where that gun is?"

"No," said Archie. "But I've a pretty good idea that I can find out."

Friedman's manner became sly and taunting. "How can you find out? I think you're a liar. What do you think of that?"

Archie turned wearily away. "Think what you like," he said. He sat down on one of the wooden chairs and looked past them toward the barred window.

"Come on," Fred said. "Let's sign that statement. What if he does find the gun? Besides, he's lying."

Friedman produced a clean white handkerchief, wiped his throat with it and sat down in the other chair. "Not so fast, my friend. There may be more to this than you think." He put the handkerchief away. "I've got my own position to think of. With such an attitude, how do I know he won't contradict your claim that you saw Giordano take the gun? If he forces the case to a trial, then the whole deal's off." He turned suddenly to Archie. "Tell me—is that your intention?"

"I certainly intend to deny that Fred could have seen Giordano take the gun," Archie said.

Chapter 19

In claiming that he knew how he could put his hands on the gun, Archie had told the truth. He realized that he didn't need the gun if his purpose was merely to contradict Fred's statement. His desire to obtain the weapon sprang from some inner urge that was obscure even to himself. It was only as an afterthought that he had realized that in obtaining the gun after the police had failed to do so, his competence as a witness for the defense would be increased. He was aware also that there was a certain absurdity about his actions, but now that he understood what had been going on in Giordano's mind, he was determined to present the truth, regardless of the consequences to himself. He felt that what he had to gain from this course had a moral value far in excess of any penalty he might incur. He would prevent Fred from signing that statement by, first, asking Giordano what he had done with the gun. And Giordano would tell him what he had refused to tell the police because, unlike the police, Archie would know how to ask. Then he would present the gun to the prosecutor with the announcement that he was in possession of evidence that denied any possible statement in which Giordano was alleged to have been seen taking the gun. This would not, of course, exculpate Giordano, but at least the facts would be presented truthfully. Besides, he simply had to know what had happened to that gun. It was as if the gun contained some final clarifying fact that he could not possibly do without. Archie's firm decision now enabled him to take a detached view of things. He looked at Friedman, seated on his right, his crispness shed like the skin of an onion and the raw personality exposed. Fred stood uncomfortably with his hand on the door knob, unable to make up his mind whether he could risk bullying Friedman into accepting his own certainty that Archie had lied.

Archie could even marvel at his feeling of separation from the problem. At the same time, he wished to make clear that his battle was not with them—that he bore no ill will. "I know this is a nuisance for you, Friedman," he began. "But try to think. What's really involved in this for you? How much does it amount to, after all? I'm the one who's willing to stand trial. What have you got to lose?"

Friedman shook his head. "He asks me what's involved. I don't understand that kind of talk. I like things straight—out in the open." He bent pleading eyes on Archie. "I'm your attorney. Isn't that so? You know about the gun? Why do you hide it from me? I'm here to help you. Why—" he waved his hand in a sweeping semi-circle to signify his bewilderment, "you're even paying me for it."

"Why can't you take my word that he's lying?" Fred interrupted. "Don't I know him well enough?"

"When I do a thing, I like to do it right," Friedman said, rising. "But," he added with resignation, bestowing a reluctant backward glance on Archie. "I'll take a chance. After all, I'm not the one with the most to lose. For a client, even though he's turned against me, I'm willing to make a fool of myself."

"Come on, then," said Fred, opening the door.

The policeman who had escorted Archie from Homicide was waiting outside. "You all through with him, counselor?" he asked, indicating Archie.

"I hope to God," Friedman muttered, waving his hands above his head. He followed Fred down the hall. "We'll see," he said, "if he comes after us to the D.A.'s office."

"He won't," Fred assured him.

"Tell me, what's the matter with him? Does he get spells like that often?"

"Who cares," Fred said brusquely.

The policeman motioned to Archie who had risen. "Come on."

"Listen," Archie said. "Take me to the D.A.'s office. Do you know which assistant is in charge of this case?"

"I guess I can take you," the policeman said, looking at him with curiosity.

John Warren, the assistant district attorney, was already in conversation with Friedman and Fred when the policeman entered to announce that Archie wished to see him. Warren, somewhat surprised, since Fred had already indicated his willingness to sign the statement and close the case, reluctantly deferred to this new turn of events and asked that Archie be shown in.

Friedman, disconcerted, gave Fred a look meant to fix on him the responsibility for the forthcoming embarrassment. Fred turned away in angry confusion, avoiding Friedman's glance as he occupied himself with contemplating a framed painting of a sailing vessel being tossed about by a violent blue sea.

As Archie entered, Friedman attempted to give Warren some inkling of the former's intention and so ameliorate the awkwardness of his own position as counsel to this wayward and unorthodox client.

"This young man objects to the signing of that statement for reasons that he absolutely refuses to make clear. I'm afraid I don't know what his intentions are. But I wouldn't take any stock in his story about being able to locate that missing gun."

"Counselor, this sounds like something I haven't been informed about," Warren said, leaning back in his chair and surveying the three of them with a canny expression. "Is there something you neglected to tell me?"

"You know me better than—"

"You know," Warren continued without waiting to hear Friedman's protest, "I prepared that statement on the assumption that I was in possession of all the known facts."

Friedman again attempted to say something, but checked himself when he saw that Warren was not yet through.

"I'm doing my best to be fair to you," Warren continued. "But I expect you to be fair to me. Homicide informs me—"

"If I can say a word, Mr. Warren," Archie interrupted, uninhibited by Friedman's respect for Warren's authority. "Mr. Friedman has been entirely fair. Whatever facts he's omitted are due to my withholding them from him."

"You mean," Warren said, gazing at Archie with the look of a man who has unexpectedly found himself swallowing something indigestible, "that you haven't told everything to your own counsel?"

"That's what I've been trying to explain," Friedman interposed. "He's got some funny ideas about how these things should be handled. I wouldn't take any stock in—"

"Wait a minute, Friedman. If the young man insists on having his own say, let's hear him out." Warren looked expectantly at Archie. Fred hovered nervously in the rear, trying to avoid the assistant district attorney's gaze by using Friedman's back as a screen.

"First of all," Archie said, "no one has any right to sign that statement. No one saw Giordano take that gun."

"Hmm," said Warren. "If your friend saw Giordano take it, how can you know what he didn't tell you?"

"Let's skip all that. If you had that gun, there wouldn't be any need for that statement, would there?"

"Well, now, what do you mean?"

"I think I can get that gun for you."

"I don't think I understand your motive. It seems to me that you're only making it harder on yourself. That statement is obviously the best way out for you. So why go to all this trouble? You're not making it very easy for Mr. Friedman, either."

"I don't think you'd understand my motive, but I'll try to explain."

Warren nodded. "You people from the Village might be surprised to learn that we understand an awful lot more down here than you give us credit for. A lot of life passes through these corridors."

"So much the better," said Archie.

"Well, then explain yourself. Is anything wrong with that statement?"

"Yes—it's a lie. Maybe it's your way of doing things. You're welcome to it for whoever doesn't give a damn. I just don't like to have your way of doing things forced on me. I feel I can afford in this situation to do things my own way. The results don't really matter. That's about all there is to it."

Warren sat back and picked at his teeth with the corner of a blotter. For some moments, he watched Archie in silence as though considering whether it would be worth bothering to reply. Friedman, his arms folded, waited with an air of patient martyrdom. Warren, at length, made up his mind. He turned from Archie to the lawyer. "Friedman, you certainly picked yourself a lulu this time."

Friedman bowed his head in philosophical obeisance to the whims of destiny. "You've got to take the good with the terrible."

"Where's that gun?" Warren suddenly snapped at Archie.

"I don't know yet."

"What?" Warren turned to the lawyer. "Friedman, did you hear what he said?"

"I told you," Friedman said. "He's a case. You're wasting your time. Throw him out and let's settle it with that statement."

"But I think I know how to get my hands on it," Archie said. "The gun, I mean."

"Oh, you think so, do you?" Warren mocked. "Well so do the police. What about it?"

"If you let me have a half hour with Giordano," Archie went on, unperturbed, "I'm certain he'll tell me where to find that gun. I can almost guarantee it."

Warren rose. "He's a nut, Friedman. He wants to stick his head in a noose. Every once in a while, one like him comes along. All right—if he wants to stick his head in a noose, I'm going to let him—just for the hell of it. I want to see this through. I'm a man that's always willing to learn." He turned to Archie. "You can have that half hour," he said. "But remember, that's the last favor you get from me."

"Thanks," Archie said.

"After that," Warren added, "you're on your own."

"That goes double for me," said Friedman.

Chapter 20

The shadow formed by the sunlight striking the barred window had crawled upward along the wall until it lay athwart a brown water stain produced by slow seepage from the ceiling. Lying on his cot, Giordano had observed that gradual ascent since morning. He had slowly come to anticipate the meeting of those two isolate forms along the stark, whitewashed wall: the geometric shadow and the amorphous stain. Something was about to be revealed by that coalescence of opposites. It carried, somehow, the merging elements of his own fate.

As the area of wall separating stain and shadow impalpably diminished, he felt an increasing excitement. The sounds of life drifting in through the cell door became amplified. The chemical odor given off by the aluminum utensils in which his food had been brought seemed to linger and grow stronger in his nostrils. The scrape of a footstep rose to a roar. The air was heavy. The whitewashed wall was too bright. The opening of the cell door sounded like an explosion.

He put his hands to his ears and turned his face to the wall. The sounds had altered and he thought of a phonograph record incredibly accelerated. His name, barely intelligible, was being repeated over and over again. He turned quickly and saw Archie standing over him. Outside, the guard was locking the cell door.

"Joe, were you asleep?"

Giordano did not answer. For some moments he continued to lie still and watch his visitor. Then a persistent ticking sound drew his attention. In an effort to locate its source, the painter let his eyes travel downward from Archie's face, past the gray front of his jacket. Just below the sleeve of the left hand a leather band protruded and he was able to make out the lower metallic edge of the other's wrist watch as a bright glint against the strap's dull surface.

"Joe."

The painter carefully swung his legs to the floor and sat up, covering a yawn with one hand and blinking with the dizziness brought on with his shift from the horizontal. "What time is it?"

Archie overlooked the cunning note in Giordano's voice. He raised his left hand and pulled back his sleeve. "Just after two," he said.

Giordano nodded with satisfaction. So it was a wrist watch. He looked into Archie's anxious face. "What are you doing here?"

"I just came from Warren's office. He's given me a half hour. I've got to talk to you."

"Warren?" Giordano repeated, searching his memory. "Who's Warren?"

"The assistant district attorney. Don't you know him?"

Giordano turned his head toward the cell door and suddenly smiled. "Oh—yes. Sure. I know him. Miserable little man, isn't he?"

Archie made an impatient movement and returned again to his original position. "I suppose so. But anyway—"

"He didn't have any shoes," Giordano said reminiscently. "I felt sorry for him. I tried to give him mine. That's a funny thing, isn't it?"

Chapter 20

Archie felt his throat tighten. He stared fearfully at the top of Giordano's bent head. Then he grasped the painter by the shoulders and began to shake him. "Joe—snap out of it, will you? Come on!"

"Hey!" Giordano exclaimed. He pushed Archie away and looked up. "Don't do that. I'm hardly awake yet. Say, how'd you get in here anyway?"

"I just told you. The assistant D.A. gave me a half hour to talk to you."

"Well, that was nice of him." He patted a space beside him on the mattress. "Sit down. What's in it for him? Or is he a special buddy of yours?"

"Look, Joe. I've only got a half hour."

"All right, sit down. Whose half hour have they given you—theirs or mine?"

"What?" Archie said, settling alongside the painter. Then he added: "Oh, I'm afraid it's theirs." He tried to smile.

"Welcome to my two-by-four universe," Giordano said. "It's too bad you won't be able to stay for the weekend. It's a great place for meditation. What fantasies I've been having."

"Listen," Archie said. "You've got to help me out. I came here—"

"Why does everybody want help?" Giordano demanded. "Wait," he said, raising his hand as Archie was about to protest, "I'll tell you. You know why? Because I've uncovered the great mystery that everybody bats his brains out over. I've got it all worked out. They can see it in my face. All right. That's one thing. But I can't just pass the secret out. You understand that?"

"Joe," Archie said. "Of course. I know it isn't that kind of secret. That's why I'm here. You've got to tell me about that gun. I must know where it is."

"Christ, is that why they sent you? Didn't they tell you?" He looked at Archie commiseratingly. "I don't remember."

"You've got to understand me," Archie said. "I'm not doing this for the police. This is all my idea. Look, let me explain. They've got you in here for killing Phil White. They think you've got to pay for that. But you and I are the only ones who know that when you knocked Phil off, you were really paying for something else. Right?"

Giordano regarded Archie with surprise. "That's very good," he said gravely. "I didn't realize—" He suddenly rose from the cot, took a few steps to the end of the cell and turned back. "Tell me what I was paying for. Can you do that?"

"Wait," Archie said. "First let me tell you what happened."

"You know what irritates me," Giordano said unexpectedly. "That half hour. It's an insult to paranoia. They put a time limit on you. Normal time, not loony time. Take a psychiatrist—a guy that's supposed to understand these things. But what does it mean, understanding it from the outside? They tell you you're loony and then they give you a half hour of their time. How am I supposed to go by their time when I tick in loony time? It's crazy," he added, grinning suddenly.

"Never mind all that," Archie said. "What's the sense in bothering with it? Let me explain what happened."

"Don't rush me," Giordano said. "I've got to stick to my own pace. That's why I've decided to go loony."

Archie slapped a fist into his palm. "That's exactly what I wanted to say." His voice rose excitedly. "You put your finger right on it when you said your own pace. Look, a guy can't go on forever at someone else's pace. He reaches a point where he's got to prove to himself that he exists. You know that crack you made to the doctor last night that the really important thing was not to create something new but to create what already exists? That was the first time I understood why you killed Phil White."

"Did I say that?" Giordano said.

Chapter 20

"When I discovered a few days ago that I was facing the chair, I told you, I went crazy. I was really scared. Remember? Then I got the idea that death didn't have to be something that was happening to me. Because I really had something to say about what it would be like. My whole empty existence didn't just have to happen to me either. Because I could accept that as a part of myself too."

"Go on," Giordano said. "You're going great. You're really in there."

"Why was I so scared when Phil White dropped dead at my feet in the 16 Bar? If I'd killed him myself, I couldn't have felt any different. I actually felt responsible. Because I didn't have any way of separating myself from it. I'd just drifted in there without any clear reasons, without exactly knowing why. If I'd known why, I would have been clear about where my responsibility ended. But I didn't know. So I felt guilty about Phil White. You didn't, even though you were the real killer. Because you really wanted to kill him. You did it without any reservations. Straight out. But there's only one thing I don't understand—"

"Every time I think of that bastard," Giordano said. "Sticking me with a load of catnip—"

"Joe—listen to me—"

"No! Get to the part about the gun."

"All right," Archie said. "This is something we can be clear about. There's a gun—a twenty-two pistol. I've got to have it. And here's why. They just tried to get me to sign a statement admitting that the gun was mine and that I saw you take it. That would close their case against you, and I'd get off with a suspended sentence. Well, maybe there's no real objection to that. It really was my gun, but I didn't like the way they were doing it. I refused to sign. So Fred got steamed up and decided to sign instead. To me, that would have been the same thing. It still would have been crawling along at their pace. I just couldn't do it after what I'd gone through. I've got too much to prove to myself. That's why I decided to produce the gun. You see, it won't make any difference for you if I sign the statement or if I produce the gun. But it will to me. I'm trying to create something that exists too. The same thing you're after. That's why I was so sure I could talk to you about it. I was sure you'd understand and let me know where you hid it." In his excitement, Archie had risen from the cot and had paced up and down the length of the small cell. Now he stopped before Giordano, grasping him by the shoulders.

"Well," he asked. "How about it?"

Giordano pushed him away. His face was somber. "No," he said. "I can't tell you." He turned his back on Archie and leaned against the cell door, gripping the bars with his hands as he looked out.

"Why not?" Archie said.

Giordano answered without turning around. "I can't remember. I can't take a chance on trying to remember."

"You've got to," Archie persisted.

Giordano turned defiantly. "Why?" he said. "Tell me why."

Archie regarded him gravely. "Because you still haven't finished what you started," he said slowly. "Because there was one thing you went off on. It was my gun. Not yours, you understand? Mine! And you still have to return it."

Giordano avoided Archie's gaze. "You sound just like that detective," he said. "He was trying to get something out of me too."

"That's a lie. And you know it's a lie. It's because you're trying to back out."

"No," said Giordano.

"It's true," Archie insisted.

Giordano turned again to peer out through the bars. "Why don't you leave me alone," he said.

Archie was beginning to feel an overwhelming weariness. He let his hands drop to his sides, then sat down heavily on the cot. For a few moments he remained preoc-

Chapter 20

cupied, staring listlessly across at the wall. "Maybe you're right," he said at last, in a tone of resignation. I shouldn't have come here. Just because there's a whole lot of stuff going on in my head, I didn't have to drag you in on it."

Giordano turned slowly to face Archie with an expression of concern. He was clearly disturbed by his visitor's abject attitude. He said in a propitiatory voice: "That's all right."

Archie shook his head. "I didn't have to make such a fuss about signing that statement. Christ, isn't it odd? Now that I think of it, what the hell was I trying to do? You've got enough to cope with. And here I am trying to unload all of my problems on you."

"Now wait a minute," Giordano began. "That isn't what I meant. I'm even glad you thought of me. Only—" Here he hesitated and regarded again the barred shadow which Archie's movements had now ceased to interrupt. The shadow lay fully across the water stain, forming a kind of frame, forcing the amorphous shape into a formal pattern.

"The only thing is," Giordano continued with a puzzled air, "why does everybody else have to have that gun? Why does it get so important? What is there about all of us that a pistol like that can make all these things happen? Here I am, in this rotten cage. And Phil's dead. And you sitting here tearing your guts out. And none of us really had anything to do with it. We're all victims of that gun." He grew agitated as he spoke, moving his arms and raising his voice so that its echo could be heard in the corridor.

Archie watched him with increasing discomfort. What right had he to do this? He should have left Giordano alone. He shouldn't have come.

"I was trying to pretend," Giordano went on. "Sure I wanted to keep the gun to myself. Hadn't I made it mine? But you're right. That's the one thing I've got to admit now. Once you've created something, it isn't yours any more.

Only—" He looked sadly at Archie. "Only I can't bear to give it up!"

"It's all right," Archie said awkwardly. "You don't have to give it up. You—"

Unexpectedly, Giordano hid his face in his hands and began to weep. Archie sprang up in panic.

"Don't," he said. "Forget the whole thing. I'll get out of here."

"No," Giordano said. "I can't—I can't sell out now. I was just thinking of that little man without shoes." He dropped his hands and turned a tear-stained face to Archie. "I was willing to give him my shoes. But the gun—which isn't mine— how can I tell you? It isn't yours any more, either."

"Never mind," Archie said, unable to grasp this last statement but unwilling to endure this scene any longer.

"But that's what you still have to see," said Giordano. "That the gun's not yours any more."

"I'm sorry, I don't—" Archie looked toward the cell door, anxious for the arrival of the guard.

"Which is why," Giordano continued, "I have to tell you where it is. Because," he looked with profound tenderness at Archie, "because I just couldn't stand your walking out of here now without knowing. No, I'd feel too alone."

"All right," Archie said, deeply touched. He spoke in a voice softened to a whisper. "Tell me where it is." He himself was now unaccountably on the verge of tears.

"It's in the yard," Giordano whispered. "You know the yard in back of the building my studio's in? Just under that middle window where you can look down and see that sumac tree?"

Archie nodded. "I can find it."

"I buried it next to the tree. On the side of the tree facing the building. It's not very deep. It's all wrapped up in sheets of cellophane so it shouldn't get hurt by the dampness. I sealed the cellophane around it with scotch tape."

Chapter 20

"What made you bury it like that?" Archie asked.

Giordano fell silent and looked at him strangely. Then he turned abruptly away. "Why do you want to know that?" he demanded in a voice bristling with suspicion.

"It's all right," Archie said hastily. "It doesn't matter."

Giordano faced him angrily. "Shall I tell you why you wanted to know?" A note of contempt crept into his voice.

"Well—"

"No, on second thought. I don't think I will. I don't really have to give you everything."

Archie heard footsteps approaching in the corridor. It was the guard coming to let him out. He felt deeply grateful. In a moment, he would be able to get away.

But he had done what was necessary. Now, although he hadn't come away with what he'd expected, he at least knew that he'd never have to do it again. He turned to Giordano as the guard unlocked the door.

"So long, Joe."

Giordano stood with his back to Archie. "I don't want you coming around here again," he said stiffly. "I don't want to be annoyed any more."

Archie stepped into the corridor and heard the guard locking the cell door again. He refrained from looking back.

Chapter 21

Warren could not resist glancing at the signed statement on his desk as Archie entered. The signature of Fred Birnley sprawled boldly across the bottom of the typed sheet.

After a moment he looked up and deliberately noted the preoccupied air that seemed to fix Archie's eyes on some point in the room midway between floor and ceiling. Warren waited, allowing himself another moment for his involuntary feeling of irritation to pass. Finally, he indicated a chair.

"Sit down," he said.

Archie lowered his eyes and met Warren's frank stare of dislike. Then he turned his head slowly as though that insignificant movement required an effort of will. Some inner resistance was implicit in the exaggerated attention he appeared to give to the act of locating the chair and then carefully settling himself in it.

Warren noted these symptoms of profound fatigue and felt his irritation diminishing. The monosyllabic query with which he now greeted Archie was consequently softened in tone.

"Well?" he said.

"He's in bad shape," Archie said, his voice a shade above a whisper.

Warren lifted the lid of a cigarette box and pushed it across the desk to Archie who shook his head.

"So now you know," Warren remarked as he reached for a cigarette. He watched Archie intently over the flame of his lighter. "Did he tell you where he hid the gun?"

The question by its brusqueness clearly assumed the negative. Archie sensed the implied scorn. He remained silent and gazed at Warren, seeking in his face how to frame his reply most articulately.

Warren snapped his lighter shut. "Why do you look at me like that?" he said. "When I ask a question, I expect an answer."

"I'm sorry," Archie said. "You sounded as if you knew the answer."

Warren shook his head in self-commiseration. He dropped the flat of his hand over the statement. "Tell me, Grau. What have you got against the world? I never in my life saw anyone who went around with a chip on his shoulder like you."

"It's complicated," Archie said. "I was only trying to figure out the best way of explaining myself. Try to understand me, Mr. Warren." Archie leaned forward, frowning in an effort to keep above the level of his fatigue. "There are things I've brought into this case that I know aren't of any interest to you. In a sense, I suppose they can be described as moral feelings, but—"

"Now look here, Grau," Warren interrupted. "Perhaps you don't understand your position very clearly. Anyone who can flaunt the law to the extent of keeping a loaded gun around the house, a gun which, because of your criminal irresponsibility, resulted in a murder, isn't exactly the one to preach to me about morals. It's my job to protect the public's morals through the law and I don't need any help from you. What's more, you've taken up more of my time than you've any right to. All I want from you—" Warren broke off suddenly and struck the desk sharply with his lighter. "Grau!"

Chapter 21

Archie turned his eyes from the window. "Oh, what the hell," he said. "Why not put me down as a lunatic and let it go at that. I can't listen to any more nonsense."

Warren slumped back in his chair and sighed. "Boy," he muttered. "This is one for the books." He continued to regard Archie in silence. Finally, he asked: "Tell me—doesn't it make any difference to you whether you walk out of here a free man or go to jail?"

"Certainly it makes a difference."

Warren shrugged. "I give up. You've got my sympathy, Grau. You're in a bad way. Take my advice. When you get out of here, you'd be doing a smart thing if you went to see a psychiatrist. Now, just so you won't be burdened with any more nonsense, suppose we forget all about this business of the gun. I thought it over and decided to let your friend Birnley sign the statement anyway. And that's all we need. I'm giving you a break in spite of yourself. Once the case is closed, it's closed. And as far as I'm concerned, it is closed. This office has more important things to spend its time on. As for you, as far as I can see, you're just an unfortunate crackpot. Now take my advice. When you get out of here, try to stay out of trouble."

"You mean," Archie said, "that I'm free?"

"That's right," Warren said. "And believe me, you're getting a break you don't deserve." He pointed with his index finger as Archie got to his feet. "Right through that door, Grau."

Archie opened the door. He shook his head musingly as he stepped into the corridor. What a character I'm turning out to be, he told himself.

He was puzzled now about how to proceed. There was still some step he felt he had to take. Nevertheless he derived satisfaction from the knowledge that he had adhered to his chosen course.

He went around a bend in the corridor and pressed a button for the elevator. An ache accompanied his thoughts of Giordano. Still there was nothing he could actually do for him. Why, therefore, did he persist in feeling that he continued to owe Giordano a debt? It was all so irrational. What was the debt? And how could he actually pay it off?

Overhead, the white signal globe flashed red. He stepped closer as the outer door slid open. The second door opened and he stepped into the elevator.

In one of those moments where recognition is reluctant but unavoidable, Archie found himself face to face with the detective who had worked on the case. His name was Brown, he recalled. The operator rolled the doors shut. He tipped the switch. The car shivered, then dipped smoothly into its descent.

Brown had been standing in a corner of the car, his face turned on a diagonal toward the forward corner occupied by the operator who sat on a small stool. When Archie entered, he had automatically turned toward the door, but had recognized Archie only after he had already begun to swing his head back on its original diagonal. This secured for both a few seconds to defer recognition. It was the detective who finally spoke first, drawing his hands from his pockets and stepping slightly out of his corner like a fighter advancing on his opponent at the opening of a round. "Hello," he said.

Archie found it necessary to make some overt motions of recognition. He lifted his head back and then bent it briskly forward in an exaggerated nod. At the same time he took a step backwards as if to place the other in proper focus.

"Hello," Archie replied. He moved his mouth to form an abbreviated smile and added apologetically. "I didn't recognize you."

"How's it going?" the detective asked. He sounded friendly.

"Oh," Archie shrugged. "It's just about over." He looked reflectively at the floor, smiled again and with an effort at lightness, announced: "I've just been ordered to go home and stay out of trouble."

"Glad to hear it," the detective said.

There was a pause as the car slowed to a stop and the doors opened.

"Watch your step," the operator said.

Archie left the car first and as the detective joined him, he repeated with an air of finality: "Yes, I guess it's all over now."

Brown lowered his head and thrust a hand into his pocket as he walked alongside Archie toward the building exit. "It was a strange case," he said. "No hard feelings, I hope."

"No." Archie found himself recalling the moment of arrest. He said nothing further, however, expecting that the detective had more to say.

"Anyway, I managed to get it pretty well cleaned up," Brown acknowledged. He seemed merely to be making a talking point. "You fellows sure lead a queer life over there in the Village."

They pushed through adjoining doors that led to the street. Then they turned mutually in the direction of the bus stop at the corner.

"It's too bad about Giordano," the detective added. "He was a character. Was he really a good artist?"

"Yes," said Archie.

"I hear he had a breakdown."

Archie examined Brown's face as he recalled Giordano's comment that he and the detective were alike. A feeling of friendliness impelled him to say: "You must've had a pretty strange time yourself."

"I'll tell you the truth. I had some funny moments. The first time I went to see Giordano, he really had me going. You'd almost think lunacy was catching—"

"Not quite," Archie said. "I think a lunatic can be like a mirror. You look at a lunatic too closely and you can see yourself there. At least, that's how I've got it figured out. I never really saw what Giordano himself looked like until a little while ago. It was—"

They had reached the bus stop when the detective turned suddenly, moving backward toward the curb as he asked in surprise: "You saw him?"

Archie nodded. "They let me see him so I could get him to tell me what he did with that gun. The police never did find it. But I guess you know."

"I know." Brown licked at his lips and watched Archie curiously. "How'd you make out?"

Archie shrugged. "That's complicated too."

"Look," said the detective. "You don't mind my being curious, do you?

"No," Archie said. "Why should I give a damn? He told me where he hid the gun all right."

"So they did find it."

"No, I didn't tell them."

In response to Brown's puzzled look, Archie added: "They weren't interested. Warren told me he considered the case closed."

"Then—is the gun still hidden?"

"As far as I know, it is."

Brown was thoughtful. "I've got a funny itch to see it," he said. "Even though the case is closed, I have to admit, I'm curious."

"I can see that."

"Are you going to do anything about that gun?"

Archie stepped off the curb as he saw the bus approaching. "Here it comes," he said.

"Where are you headed now?"

"Home, I guess. No, I'm not going home either. I wanted to drop in at the 16 Bar for a drink."

"The 16 Bar," the detective repeated with a little nod.

"You have any place special to go now? Would you like to join me?"

Chapter 21

The detective hesitated. "There's not much point."

"Are you on duty now?"

"No, but—"

"Then come along. Come on, act like a human being. The case is settled. But a few other things aren't." Archie signaled the bus as he spoke.

"What few other things?"

"Ride up with me," Archie said. "I'll tell you."

The bus had stopped. Archie climbed aboard. The detective remained hesitant, but he followed anyway.

Chapter 22

The afternoon sunlight had settled listlessly inside the 16 Bar and lay in a pallid broad band across the walnut counter. From here it ascended the inside wall and clung in broken, venous strands along the rows of bottles. The bartender sat alone on a stool near the window. The light fell over his shoulder to the newspaper he had spread out on the bar. Overhead, the stilled blades of the two rotary fans seemed to droop. As Archie entered with the detective, it seemed to him that an odd peace pervaded the place. It was like the peace of exhaustion. The atmosphere was one of aftermath.

"Well, what do you know," the bartender exclaimed.

"Hi, Carlo," Archie said. "Don't work too hard."

Carlo folded the paper, lifted the barboard and stepped behind it. "What's the matter? You give up sleeping in the daytime?"

"Sure, I'm going through a change of life. I'm going to settle down and marry a nice schoolteacher."

""Maybe it'll do you good," Carlo said. "Only you'll have to go to work."

"Who said I don't work?"

"That writing racket—you call it work?" Carlo turned to the detective who leaned on the bar with his elbows.

"Maybe you can tell me. If he sleeps all day and comes in here all night, when does he find time to work?"

"I work on Sundays," Archie said. "Once in a while, anyway."

"You said it," Carlo declared. He looked from one to the other. "What'll it be?"

"Two beers," said Archie.

Carlo drew the beers and placed them on the counter. "Where's Fred? I ain't seen him all week."

"You haven't seen me either."

Carlo reflected. "That's right. You ain't been in here since the night Phil White— Hey, what's this about that crazy artist, Giordano? Did he really do it?"

Archie and Brown exchanged glances. "I guess he did," Archie said, staring down at his beer.

"What for? That's what I can't figure out. Did they have a fight about something?"

"I don't know," Archie said.

Carlo shook his head. "Boy, is this a place. I can never figure out nothing that goes on down here."

Archie sipped at his beer. Then he set his glass down and looked at the detective. "What's the matter?" he asked.

The detective hadn't touched his beer. "I was just thinking about the whole thing. It wasn't such a small affair when you get right down to it. Take this guy Giordano. You know what I mean?"

Archie squinted as the afternoon sunlight shifted. "That's one of the unsettled things on my mind. Maybe I'm just making a mystery out of him. Maybe I'm sentimental. But I can't help believing there was something big he was trying to get across. I don't know. I feel sad when I think about it."

"Why sad?"

Archie made a vague movement with his shoulders. "Just sad. God, he was beautiful the last time I saw him."

Chapter 22

"I guess losing your mind is sad. But what can anybody do about it? On my job, you run into worse things. After a while you learn to toughen up. Or you don't last."

Archie smiled wanly. "I suppose there's something in that."

He saw that Carlo had returned to his newspaper. He pushed his beer aside and got up. "Let's get out of here."

The detective dropped some change on the counter. "Sure," he said. "Let's go."

Carlo looked up as they started out. "What's the matter with the beer?"

"The beer's all right," Archie said. "But I've got work to do."

They went out and by tacit consent began walking north along Seventh Avenue.

"What a crum joint," the detective commented after they'd gone about a block.

"It's pretty lively at night," Archie explained.

"I guess it is."

"I've been going in there for years. Ever since I've lived down here."

"I never knew there was a yard in back of Giordano's place," said the detective.

"Neither did I. I thought it was a regular loft building."

"Some of these old buildings are something."

"I can't figure out why I used to go in there every night for so long," Archie said.

"The 16 Bar? A bad habit. Just happens. Some guys, their whole lives are habits."

"When we were in there just now, I felt so funny and stiff. Making jokes with Carlo. Like a vaudeville routine."

"You're still jumpy over the whole thing."

"Probably," Archie said.

They continued walking in silence. As they approached the building where Giordano had lived, the detective remarked: "I never figured I could get so interested in a case after it was washed up."

"Better watch out," Archie said. "First thing you know, you'll be taking up painting."

"Me?" Brown snorted. "Maybe in my old age."

They entered the lobby of the building. Archie pointed out the sign with the name Giordano lettered on it. "It doesn't look as if they've rented it yet."

"There must be a door leading to the yard behind that staircase."

The elevator operator stopped them. "What are you looking for?" he asked.

"Is there a yard out there?"

"You can't go out in that yard," the operator said. Brown reached into his breast pocket and flashed his badge. The operator shook his head. "I'll show you," he said. "It's just back of the staircase."

"Never mind," Brown said. "We'll find it."

"Is there something wrong out there?"

"No, forget about it."

They proceeded past the staircase and pushed through a door that opened onto a small yard whose yellowed soil supported patches of scrubby weed. The adjacent buildings towered overhead, shutting off the sunlight. A stunted sumac tree grew alongside the rotting wooden fence about ten feet beyond the door. Heaps of litter lay scattered on the ground.

Archie pointed to a broken patch of earth near the tree. "That looks like the place," he said.

The detective picked up a large fragment that had been part of an earthenware flowerpot. "We can use this."

Archie accepted the potsherd and bent down to scrape the top layer off the patch of earth. The dry, gravelly soil came away easily. The detective bent over, watching intently as the other gradually scooped out a shallow area.

"He said he wrapped it in cellophane," Archie said.

Chapter 22

"God, now that I'm here, it seems weird. What the hell did he bury it in cellophane for?"

Archie uttered an exclamation and began wielding his impromptu spade more rapidly.

"You got it?" Brown whispered.

"That's funny," Archie murmured. He had partially uncovered what looked like a long roll. "It couldn't be a gun." He dropped the fragment and grasped the free end of the roll, pulling it loose from the soil. "What the hell is this?"

The detective stared at the cellophane-wrapped cylinder which was about the size of an ordinary rolled-up window shade. "There couldn't be any gun in that. It's not thick enough. Is there anything else?"

Archie passed the cylinder to Brown while he probed about in the hole with the potsherd. "No, there's nothing else."

"I'll be damned," the detective exclaimed. "It's a hunk of canvas. Look!"

Archie got up and noted the edge of a rolled canvas where Brown had opened the cellophane at one end. "Let me see," he said, reaching for it. He tore at the wrapping and managed after a moment to slip it off. Then he grasped the top edge of the canvas and let it unroll.

"A painting," the detective exclaimed. "Let's see." He stepped behind Archie as the latter held the painting out at arm's length and eyed it in numbed silence.

"What a guy," Brown remarked. "I don't know beans about painting. Is it good? It doesn't look much like the one at your house."

Archie moved his head slowly from side to side. He had turned very pale as he stood there staring at the canvas.

"Are you sure he said it was the gun he buried?" the detective asked.

Archie nodded and began mechanically to reroll the canvas. "Boy I'm just beginning to realize how whacky that guy was. What a thing to do," the detective commented. "He must've had a crazy idea of saving his work for the future."

Archie held the canvas cylinder gingerly in both hands. "Come on," he said quietly. "Let's go."

Brown hesitated. "Maybe we ought to look around. That gun still may be here."

"No," said Archie firmly. "There's nothing else here." He started for the building door and the other followed.

"Whatever made him tell you it was the gun he buried?" The detective appeared to be putting the question to himself.

When they reached the lobby, the elevator operator accosted them. "Did you find what you wanted?"

"We found it," the detective said. "It's nothing important."

Archie had gone ahead and the detective hurried after him, joining him on the street. "What are you going to do with it?" the detective asked, eying the canvas covetously.

"Oh—" Archie frowned. "I'll see."

"If he was really a good artist like you said," the detective continued, "it's too bad a guy like that had to lose his mind." He hesitated. "I was just thinking, if it didn't make any difference to you, I'd kind of like to have it. I thought I'd like to keep it for a souvenir."

"No," Archie said. "I think I'll keep it."

"You've already got one of his paintings," the detective said.

"I know."

"Well, I just thought—"

"I happen to know Giordano wanted me to have this," Archie said.

Brown noticed something in Archie's face. He looked away in sudden embarrassment. "Sure," he said lamely. He gazed thoughtfully along the street. "I guess I ought to be getting along."

"I think I'll head for home too," Archie said.

"Well—" The detective lifted his hand in farewell. "I suppose I'll see you."

"So long." Archie tucked the roll of canvas under his arm and began walking away.

The setting sun dropped behind a bank of clouds and the long shadows faded so that the street became gray. Archie walked slowly, his heels scuffing along the pavement. He stared into the shop windows as he passed. Then the sun reappeared and Archie saw his reflection in the glass of a furniture shop. He stopped for a moment and studied his image. He shifted the canvas to his other arm, Squaring his shoulders slightly, he looked once more in the glass, then continued toward home.

The idea had taken possession of him that, in a sense, he was Giordano's trustee, that there was still something the painter wanted to accomplish through him. It was all rather vague, of course, but Archie had a sentimental need for presuming such a relationship. His own problems had brought him so close to Giordano that he had to achieve himself what the other had failed in. Otherwise the futility of Giordano's end would always disturb him.

As he walked, he mused over what it must have been that had prompted the burial of the canvas in the earth. But, he asked himself, excited by the symbolic meaning of the act, was there not always some need for returning to their pure source those things which in being taken into man only become art in being given back again? That was what Giordano must have meant when he had exclaimed in the cell: "But the gun isn't yours anymore either." Yet Giordano had also confessed his own inability to part with the secret of the gun, as though he had learned to take into himself but not how to give back. Thus, the careful burial of the painting had been but a partial giving back. The absurdity of that cellophane wrapping! It had still been necessary for Giordano to protect what he had known he must give up and yet could not completely abandon. But finally, some feeling of brotherhood had enabled him to surrender his secret to Archie. And it was as though he expected Archie to perform that last act to which he hadn't been able to bring himself. It had struck Archie all at once on unearthing the painting instead of the gun that he had become his brother's keeper. The nature of his obligation, which now brought him almost to the verge of tears, compelled him to think through the rest of Giordano's behavior, to acquaint himself with it thoroughly, so that, while already sensing what he had to do, he could clearly understand each step that had led to his emotional conviction.

He recalled again Giordano's idea of attempting through art to rise beyond himself. Giordano had failed because of his inability to distinguish between gun and painting and life. He had confused the inside with the outside, the world with himself. Had he destroyed instead what the gun stood for, he might have been free. He would have been able to project into his art, not the gun, not the violence which he mistook for himself, but really himself. That was how the canvas had finally become the gun to Giordano. Therefore, what Giordano really wanted of him was to destroy the gun, to give it back entirely. Thus the cycle would be completed and the artistic act made whole. And Archie too would be made whole, since, in doing this for Giordano, he would also be doing it for himself.

When Archie finally reached home, the apartment was empty. But there was a depression along the length of the leather couch and one of the pillows had been placed at one end. Fred had evidently been lying there recently. The rest of the apartment was quite in order. Everything was in its proper place. The finished section of the Brankowski manuscript lay in a neat pile on the table. The typewriter lay enclosed in its case beside it. But dust seemed to have accumulated everywhere. It lay across the floor in a thin film, giving the place an abandoned air.

Chapter 22

Placing the canvas on the table next to the manuscript, Archie went into the kitchen and took some newspapers from a stack under one of the cabinets. He went into the living room and began to crumple the sheets into loose balls which which he deposited in the fireplace. Then he took the canvas from the table and placed it too inside the fireplace so that it lay across the crumpled sheets. From his pocket he drew a book of matches and proceeded to light a fire.

Settling himself on a low footstool before the fireplace, he watched the edges of the paper curl until a bright blaze arose that obscured his view of the canvas. An acrid smell filled the room as the paint burned. Archie could feel the heat on his face. His eyes smarted and filled with tears.

The roaring draft of the fire prevented his hearing the opening of the door. It was only when he heard Fred's step behind him that he turned and saw the firelight flickering on his roommate's face.

"Well, so you're back," Fred said.

"Hello," Archie said.

"What's the fire for?" Fred sniffed curiously. "What're you burning? Something stinks." He walked over to the couch, sat down and stared inquisitively across the room at Archie who had turned to gaze again into the flames which were already beginning to die down.

"By the way," Fred continued, his voice unexpectedly taking on a friendly tone. "I started to wait for you outside while you went to visit Giordano's cell. I didn't want you to think I signed that statement out of malice. Anyway, I wanted a chance to talk to you alone, without that jerk of a lawyer around. But the reason I didn't stay—"

Fred paused and began plucking nervously at his trouser crease. His head was bent toward the floor.

"What?" Archie said, without turning from the fire.

"I ran into that gay and charming couple," Fred went on. "Sylvia and Sydney. At first, they pretended not to see me. So I spoke to them. You should have seen their faces.

They looked absolutely white. They'd been to Homicide just after you were there and they'd been told they wouldn't have to appear again. Anyway, it was something. Sydney, the poor bastard, practically hid himself behind Sylvia's back, he was so scared. Oh, did she pick a guy for herself! It was a situation I wouldn't have missed for anything. I didn't say a word about what they'd done, but, in an offhand way, I pretended to be friendly. You know what I did?" Fred raised his head and chuckled.

Archie continued to listen in silence." I rode back with them on the bus," Fred chuckled. "I couldn't resist. I just had to prolong the torture. They sat there looking at me glumly while I made casual remarks about nothing in particular. By the time I left them, that poor jerk Sydney must have aged about ten years. What a scene! But anyway, I certainly showed him up. Sylvia won't ever forgive him for the way he behaved. Not if I know her." He broke off and regarded Archie who, without answering, continued to stare into the fireplace.

"What's the matter?" Fred demanded, suddenly embarrassed. "Weren't you listening?"

Archie nodded. "I was listening."

Fred sat quietly for a moment, then turned his head to one side and began to make loud sniffing sounds. "What do you need that foul-smelling fire for? What's wrong? You chilly?"

Archie shook his head. "I'm warm now," he said quietly.

Fred shrugged and placed a pillow behind himself. "Then what's the matter with you?" he asked.

"I'm all right."

"You certainly weren't all right this afternoon. What a crazy act you put on in the D.A.'s office." He was silent for an interval. Then, with a mocking smile, he asked:

"Tell me—did you find the gun?"

Chapter 22

Archie rubbed his eyes with the back of his hands. "Yes," he said. "I found it."

Fred sat up stiffly and stared. "You did? Where? What did you do with it?"

"I got rid of it," Archie said. He continued to sit and watch the glowing embers which were all that now remained of the fire.

Colophon

The Blowtop is set in Century Old Style, a long-accepted workhorse of the publishing industry designed in 1909 for the American Typefounders by Morris Fuller Benton. Chapters are opened with a Century Schoolbook variant designed, also by Morris Fuller Benton, in 1935.

These designs are based on Century, a typeface first created for the American *Century* magazine in 1896.

Designed and set in the foothills of the Adirondacks by Syllables using Adobe software which provided electronic files used directly to create negatives for printing.